Waterline

By the same author

God's Own Country

Waterline

ROSS RAISIN

VIKING
an imprint of
PENGUIN BOOKS

VIKING

Published by the Penguin Group
Penguin Books Ltd, 80 Strand, London WC2R ORL, England
Penguin Group (USA) Inc., 375 Hudson Street, New York, New York 10014, USA
Penguin Group (Canada), 90 Eglinton Avenue East, Suite 700, Toronto, Ontario, Canada M4P 2Y3
(a division of Pearson Penguin Canada Inc.)
Penguin Ireland, 25 St Stephen's Green, Dublin 2, Ireland
(a division of Penguin Books Ltd)
Penguin Group (Australia), 250 Camberwell Road,
Camberwell, Victoria 3124, Australia (a division of Pearson Australia Group Pty Ltd)
Penguin Books India Pvt Ltd, 11 Community Centre,
Panchsheel Park, New Delhi – 110 017, India
Penguin Group (NZ), 67 Apollo Drive, Rosedale, Auckland 0632, New Zealand
(a division of Pearson New Zealand Ltd)
Penguin Books (South Africa) (Pty) Ltd, 24 Sturdee Avenue,
Rosebank, Johannesburg 2196, South Africa

Penguin Books Ltd, Registered Offices: 80 Strand, London WC2R ORL, England

www.penguin.com

First published 2011

1

Copyright © Ross Raisin, 2011

Set in 12/14.75pt Dante MT Std
Typeset by Jouve (UK), Milton Keynes
Printed in Great Britain by Clays Ltd, St Ives plc

A CIP catalogue record for this book is available from the British Library

ISBN: 978–0–670–91735–8

I

One here, a soft fog of flowers painted on the front.

There's plenty more like that, plus as well the wild flower kinds. Meadows. Bustling hedgerows. A woodland clearing mobbed with bluebells. Hard to imagine there's this many types of card in the supermarket. A churchyard, quiet and peaceful with brown leaves blowing about. A teddy bear. And another here that's for some reason a cat gazing out the window at a sea view.

It's Robbie that wanted to put the cards up. He wasn't much wanting to do it himself, but Robbie had dug the heels in. What else are you going to do with them? Stick them in a drawer? Leave them lying on the counter with the funeral programmes and the electric bills? So now the pair of them are in the corridor, fixing them up to the red ribbon that Robbie's fished out from the Christmas cardboard box. The light dimming in the front door. Dull laughter from the living room, where the rest of them are sat watching the television.

'You know all these people, Da?'

'No really, being honest. There were some the day even, I don't know who they were. A few would've been from the department store. And then the family, course.' He nods at the living room wall. 'I preferred no to ask.'

Robbie is reading inside a card. 'They could've introduced themselves,' he says, closing the card and pegging it with a red plastic Christmas tree. It's normally the wife does this, getting up the greetings cards. This same red ribbon drooping off the pictures about the living room; pinned-up spruce as launch bunting around a ship, dutifully awaiting the chop from whichever of the wee begrudging women of the royalty have been sent up.

There's going to be too many cards will fit in the lobby and corridor. Robbie asks will they get up the rest in the living room when Alan and Lynn are away to their bed. No, he tells him. He isn't having these cards all about the room when Robbie and Craig are sleeping in there. No that it makes a great deal of sense but. When everything else in the room is some kind of reminder. Fact is, if you start taking down all the things in the place that are fingered with memories, then that's the whole house emptied.

Dear Mick,

Words don't say enough. If there's anything we can do, please let us know. All our thoughts are with you the now.

Love from Derek and Jean and all the family

One thing you can be sure, it's the women that have written them. Nay chance any of this coming from the husbands. All our thoughts are with you the now. No that it should be but, no that it should be. It was the same story earlier: the women all hats and hands and kind words while the husbands stood in beside them, cloyed up. He would've been the same but. No denying it. Silent, listening politely while Cathy said everything that was needed. These were men like him, guys he'd worked with, easier with steel sparks showering on top their head and their mate pattering bullshit in their ear. You can't blame them. As natural to them, a funeral, as redundancy. And the response aye the same: straight to the bar, boys.

'I was talking to Claire,' Robbie says. 'You know, was with Maw at the store?'

'I mind her, aye.'

'She was saying how bad they all took it when they heard. Says the place hasn't been the same the last year.' He looks round at the living room door and says in a quieter voice, 'She couldn't understand Lynn's stupid finger food either. Serious, what was all that about?'

'I missed out on it.' He takes a peg from the box and looks up at Robbie. 'They're trying to help, Rob, that's all.'

'Come off it, Da. Mozzarella fucking parcels? In the Empress? Fuck off. There was a whole black bag left afterwards at their end of the table.'

True enough. He'd actually watched Desmond clearing it out

afterwards, when everyone had went. A quick sniff and a nibble of Lynn's various parcels, weighing up the resale possibilities, before dumping them in the bag.

Mick had kept himself in with the main group, huckled together at one end of the spread by the sausage rolls and the cheese sandwiches, Robbie and his wife either side of him like a pair of minders. Craig keeping to himself, away in a corner. Truth be told, he wouldn't've objected trying one of Lynn's mozzarella parcels, but it would have meant going over the other side of the table, where Alan and Lynn were holding court with the rest of Cathy's family. Most of they lot he hadn't even seen since the wedding; so you're talking thirty-five years ago. And that's the ones that came. Some of these he'd probably never clapped eyes on in his life. He'd gave a bye to the idea of going over. Leave that lot to themselves, he thought.

It was only the weans, scootling about the place, who moved between the two groups. And the brother-in-law, of course. Man of the people Alan there, he didn't miss his opportunity to introduce himself. Heartfelt greetings to the ones he knew – quite a few of them from back in the day in the yards – never mind it was him who'd bloody laid them off. Christsake. Smiling away there. No hard feelings, eh? We didn't want to do it but see that was the times, there was no choice.

Mick had made sure to keep his distance. Took himself away for a pee when it looked one moment Alan was coming over to speak to him. When he'd closed the lavvy door behind, he saw that Desmond had gave a proper clean in there. There were toilet rolls stacked in the windowsill, and he'd moved the rotten rolled carpet that used to be outside the window. The blockages cleared from the urinals. A few extra pineapple-soap chunks. Strange how it goes but that was probably the only moment all day when he was close to greeting, when he saw that. He stood there a moment after he'd finished peeing and for a few seconds just, something got hold of him and it was an effort to stop the tears coming on. This pure strong feeling that you could only describe as utter gratefulness toward the guy because he'd cleaned out his toilets.

When he came back out, the brother-in-law had moved away, his big broad shape over on the other side of the room, doing the rounds. He was like a politician. Getting into the group at the bar, shaking hands, making sure everybody knew it was him had paid for it all.

Robbie is looking at him. 'It wasn't on either' – he jerks his head at the wall – 'that speech of his.'

Mick doesn't respond. He pegs up another card, overlapping them as they get near the end of the corridor.

'He barely mentioned you. Craig and me, sure, but anybody could've listened to that and thought you and Maw had never met – that she'd lived her whole life up in the Highlands with the sons of fucking lairds chasing after her. She'd have skelped him, if she'd heard it.'

He goes in the box for one of the last tree pegs. He isn't getting into this the now. No with the guy sat there in the next room. He keeps quiet, and the two of them get on with the job in silence a while.

'Sorry, Da, I don't mean it like that. It's just, mean, he's a bloody blowhard.'

'Robbie.'

'I know, sorry.'

They have done along both sides of the corridor. There is a small stretch just, by the living room door, left to fill.

'I'll put these up in the kitchen somewhere,' Robbie says, holding up his last handful. He walks off, and Mick stands a few seconds looking down the two lines of cards. The sound of the television gets louder, fades away again. There are two cards next to each other, he notices, identical. Foggy flowers in a vase. Intrigued a moment, he steps forward to get a look who they're from.

Pete and Mary; Don and Sheila. He must have opened these cards himself sometime over the last few days, but he hadn't took full notice of the names. Both couples were there the day. There hadn't been much chance to talk but it was good to see them. Familiar faces. The men bloodshot and bald the now but aye familiar. He sees Pete now and then because they stay no that far away still, but Don, he couldn't have seen him in twenty years. Twenty-one, in fact. He can mind fine well actually the last time he saw him: they were in the Empress, the same stools they'd been stuck to for months, fuck this, fuck that, fuck the brother-in-law, fuck Thatcher, fuck the dunny money, bastards. But they'd took their dunny money and by then they'd drunk most of it, and the last he saw of Don he was steamboats and drawling how him and the wife were moving out of the city. They were back the now, they told him. Found themselves a nice done-up flat in a tenement in Drumoyne, where the landlord wasn't quite the robber their last one was.

The wives must have read about Cathy in the *Southside News*. Went to the Co and plumped for the same card. He imagines Mary and Sheila going in for it, putting it on the counter with a paper, pack of fags, Lotto ticket.

He gives Pete and Mary's card a read:

Mick,

We were so very sorry to hear about Cathy. She was such a wee gem. I still mind fine well the launch days and the pair of us dressed up in our finest, and you and Pete three sheets to the wind! Pete is working on the crane at the old John Brown yard at the moment, of all places. I know the last year must have been very hard on you and the family, Mick. If there's anything at all we can do,

All our best,
Pete and Mary

He smiles. She does go on, Mary. He puts the card back up on the ribbon. He's heard about the crane. Turned into a visitor centre. He's seen it lit up pink and red at night a couple of times when he's been over near Clydebank. The last he knew, they were talking about putting a restaurant in the jib and making it revolve. He'd read that in the paper. It was part of a project to represent the industrial heritage of the area. A revolving pink restaurant. You've got to wonder how they dream these things up. And see the view? That's one thing for starters they'll have to change. All very well getting the full panorama but if all you're looking out on is a puddled wasteland every direction – gangs of weans playing football and smoking, pigeons roosting and crapping over the rusted fabrication sheds – it isn't going to make your mozzarella parcels taste much the better, is it?

In the kitchen Robbie has put up the cards on top of the microwave. He takes the last lot out of Mick's hand and arranges them in with the others. Through the wall, next door's baby is wailing. Mick leans against the counter and looks out the window at the back garden, the tubs of flowers that have gone thin and yellow, overgrown.

'Don't feel ye've got to stay, Robbie,' he says.

'We'll stay as long as we can, it's no bother. Anyway, Christ, we've come that far, there's no point us leaving yet.'

'I know that. But Jenna will want to get back soon. It's no right spending too long away when they're that age.'

'He's fine at his grannie's. Knowing Jenna's maw, she's probably teaching him how to make homebrew or go tracking through the bush.' He balances the last card on top of the microwave. 'Anyway, we're not leaving you on your own with the Highlanders.' He is grinning. 'How long do they plan stopping, you know?'

He's about to tell him he isn't sure, they haven't said, but just then the sound of the television comes loudly from the corridor. There are footsteps, which pause a moment, then continue toward the kitchen. Craig comes in the room without speaking or looking at either of them, and opens the fridge. He crouches, looking inside the door, but he obvious can't find what he wants and starts moving aside the packs of sausages on the bottom shelf.

'After a beer, son?'

He doesn't reply. Keeps looking, next shelf up.

'They're in the carrier on the side here, if ye are.'

He gets up, giving a quick look at the cards on the microwave. Then he goes for a can out of the bag over by where Robbie is standing.

'Thanks,' he says, snapping the can open as he leaves the room.

He wakes and looks out the window at the dark. A few wee lights on in a few distant multis. It's awful warm but. He considers a moment getting out of the bed to open a window, and stays a while trying to work up the energy to go do it, but in the end he gives it a miss and stays put where he is. Ye buried the wife today. She died, and ye buried her. Somehow it's no registering. He repeats it to himself a few times, but it's as though the words don't make sense, he can't get understanding them. What he feels instead is the same as he felt the day last week the hospital telephoned to say she'd passed away. Relief, is what it is. It is a relief the funeral's over, that it's went off okay; Craig didn't put the mix in; he doesn't have to talk to Alan about arrangements any more. He doesn't have to imagine her in another bed somewhere while he's lying here. Course there's other things he could be imagining but they're so far off seeming real they're out in fucking hyperspace. He turns over, sticky, heavy and sticky. It was hot the day too. Obvious enough they were all sweaty and tickling in their hats and their suits, but what can you do – it's a funeral.

He kept off saying it earlier, but he's really hoping Robbie and Jenna will stay a while longer before they disappear back to Australia. That he won't be left alone with these more testy elements of the household. Although surely the Highlanders won't be here much longer. There's nothing for them to do now that the funeral is over, and there's nay danger Lynn is wanting to stop around enjoying the luxuries. Craig – that's another story. And not one that he's too keen sharing, that's clear enough. He's here the now because Robbie's told him he has to be here, and probably he'll be away as soon as Robbie's gone. No that Yoker is the other side of the world, but the way he's acting it's fine well possible that it'll be Robbie that's back here again first. He needs to talk with him. Go for a drink. Find out what's going on in that brainbox of his. They both of them need to do that. And if they do, maybe best for his own part swerving the fact he's no greeted once since she died; that all he can think is: it's a relief, and when are all of these lot going to get out of the house.

2

The multis stand solid in a row like a picket line, looking down over the red tenement streets filing toward the Clyde. From up on the seventeenth storey, the view's a beauty. You can see the glimmering glass roof of the Botanical Gardens north of the river. Kelvingrove Park. The Exhibition Centre's silver armadillo. And further on, the skyline of the Campsie Fells, keeping the city in. Joe doesn't much look out at these things though. If he's looking out, it'll be at Ibrox. The ground's a few minutes' walk from the multi just. On match days, he can see the supporters coming in from all around, crowds growing on the pavements outside the pubs, pouring in through the streets.

This morning but he's having a see out the window as the sun comes up. Watching the dismal light peter in through the streets that run straight lines toward the river, bending only where they have to go around the stadium, or broken where they've took out the tenements and no got round to replacing them. By the river, there's the twinkling new apartment blocks at Glasgow Harbour, the dry ski centre, and down the water, the shipyards, what's left of them. Govan, this near side; Scotstoun, across the water. From where he is, he can just make out the top of HMS *Defender*, sat at her berth at Govan. She looks from up here like an Airfix model, with her miniature gun and helicopter pad on the flight deck. That's where Joe is headed, the light nearly up now and him away out the flat, clicking shut the front door to go pick up Suggie.

It is six o'clock. There's never anybody about in the building now except for one queer old ticket he sees on the stair sometimes, who gets up to give his dog a walk. It isn't so bad, this time in the morning. He's tired, but it's fine. The back shift is the one that kills him. He presses the button and the lift doors are straight open. They cleaned it out a week or two ago, so it's no bogging like it was, but it's been wrote on already. CUNT, one wall says, nice and simple. He gets out on the ninth floor and goes toward Suggie's.

He chaps the door. There's a light on underneath. A good sign. He's tired enough himself this time the morning, but he's pure sparkling compared to Suggie. There's times he'll be banging five minutes before there's any answer, and a couple of mornings he's resorted to giving it a wee clang with the fire extinguisher off the wall fixing. The door's looked better, in truth. Today though Suggie opens it on the second knock. He's in his pants still, but he's up.

'Come in, mate.'

Joe follows him in and sits on the settee while Suggie goes in the bedroom to get dressed. The television is on and he looks at it without paying much attention. There's a fair number of empty cans about, on the table, over the floor. Suggie must've had some mates round. No the less, he's dressed quick enough, appearing at the bedroom door in a couple of minutes, red eyes, grinning, his yellow helmet in his hand.

'Right, we off, well?'

Once onto the street the two apprentices get making their way briskly through the crisp cool morning toward the yard. They go over Saturday's match again, a couple of times, but most of the way they walk without talking. The roads are near deserted. A few cars. The old boy from their block, coming back with his dog. They give him a nod.

It wasn't always like this, course. Their fathers and their grandfathers have shown them enough photographs – photographs there's plenty of in the grand crumbling library they are walking past now – how it used to be. These same streets a hundred years ago, sixty, forty even, mobbed with hundreds of workers starting out for the day shift. Tired and quiet, like this pair, getting moving. The noise of boots on the road, the hooter about to sound up the way and signal the start of work. The occasional wife in a tenement window in her nightdress, watching her man off, and him finding his way into his own team, grouping up as they move on – riveters, caulkers, blacksmiths, the welders clear visible in their spotted hats and their leathers, boilermakers, platers – the whole black squad marching on up the road. And at the back, the apprentices, pishing about.

A different story the now. Two lads in blue overalls walking through the empty streets like a pair of convicts who've just survived the end of the world; passing by the primary school, the park, the red-stone tenements, and the terraces of grey pebble-dash houses with their wee patches of front garden.

One of these, the grass growing longer than its neighbours, has a great flash Saab parked bold as day out the front. Inside, Mick is listening to the brother-in-law snoring loudly through the wall. He's put them in the boys' old room, so they will be lying there asleep across the way from each other, the two beds having been pushed years ago as far apart as possible. The sound he's making, Alan must be on this side closest to himself. If there'd been anywhere else to put them, he'd have put them there, but there wasn't, simple as that. So they'll have to put up with it just, staying in a weans' room. Nothing has changed in there since Robbie was eighteen and he moved to Australia – it'd hardly changed in fact for a long time before that – the opposing walls still covered with football stickers and Blu-Tack scabs, a great worn circle of carpet between the two beds, faded from years of board games and fighting.

He turns over, toward the window. The snoring unrelenting. Christsake. The man can't keep quiet even when he's asleep.

Down the stair in the living room, Robbie will be slumbering on the floor with an arm curled around the wife. They are on a pile of stale brown blankets Robbie found from somewhere. No that they two mind. They don't. They're fine. On the other side of the room the older brother lying there in his sleeping bag and his legs poking out from the end of the settee. Thinking his thoughts. Thinking his thoughts and keeping the lot of them to himself.

The truth is, it is good of the Highlanders to have come. They could have drove down for the funeral and then been away back to their lochside and their mighty brick stronghold and that would've been that, never to be seen again. They don't have to be here. It is Alan's choice that they are. That's obvious enough, the way she pin-pricks around the house. The peeved squeezed eyeballs every time she gets inspecting a piece of cutlery or a glass out the cupboard. Go on, well, Lynn, what is it ye think, eh? Because ye're no making it quite clear enough with the subtle facial movements there. Ye think it's a dump, eh? Well go on, then, and get to fuck why don't ye?

The snoring has stopped. For a few minutes, the house is peaceful. A thin shaft of light is through the curtains, falling on the carpet at the bottom of the bed. After a while though, the snoring starts up again, quiet at first, then gaining force. See another way you could look at it: he's retired a long while the now, so an event like this isn't exactly getting in the way of things for them. They can make space for times like this. Births, deaths, the graduation of the miraculous son, no able sadly to make it yesterday because he's over in America, making his millions, how lovely for him.

As well, their summer holiday is by. A trip to France this year, cycling round the vineyards and taking photos of each other in food markets examining the local sausagemeats. He shouldn't be so hard on them. It can't be easy of course for the brother-in-law either, let's no forget, the responsibility he's got to shoulder. The responsibility he's aye got to shoulder.

Mick gets out of bed. It's early still and everyone else will be asleep, but he goes in the bathroom to wash his face, puts on a short-sleeve shirt and trousers, and steps down to the kitchen. He checks in the cupboard to see if there's any bread left, but it's been finished, so he closes the cupboard door and sits down at the table, looking out the window, where a wee disappointed sparrow is hopping about the grass wondering how there's nay food put out for him these days.

So this is grief, well. Sat at the kitchen table with all your joys and your miseries sleeping and snoring about you and you sat there wondering what to do for your breakfast. Maybe it's by, maybe that's it, he's gone through ten months already and the moment when she's dead actually marks the end of it because she's gone now, she's no laid there dying in front of him one day to the next. It's over. He'd greeted back then, alright, when they'd been told. On his own, or the pair of them together sat clutching to each other at this same table. That day the doctor phoned them up and asked could they both please come in to see him. The X-ray results were returned. It wasn't her back. Pleural mesothelioma. A total white-out of her left lung. A year, maybe, at the most. He closes the eyes and tries picturing her, her face, before that, while she looked healthy still. It's a blank but, the brain doesn't want to go there, so he sits with the eyes closed just. A moment of peace. You keep on. What else can you do? You keep on.

Down on the floor by the bin he notices a box of cereal. He picks it up, gets himself a bowl and shakes out the last flakes and the sawdust from the bag inside. The Highlanders are going the messages later, they announced last night, so there will be plenty enough food for them all soon enough, even the wee chap outside, given up and flown off the now. It'll be organic, course, but such is life, eh. Him and the sparrow aren't complaining.

Above his head, somebody is walking about. He puts the box back by the bin and gets the kettle on, returns to his seat at the table. And again, the same thought that keeps coming back: he is alive. He's the picture of bloody health sat at the kitchen table. The floor creaks again above his head. And no just him as well, still alive.

That evening they all sit in the living room with the television on, eating the spaghetti Bolognese that Lynn has made. Everybody agrees it is good and tasty, except for Lynn, who says it should have garlic and it should have tomato purée and it should have whatever else in it. She hadn't thought to get these things when she was in the supermarket. If she'd known there was none in the house she would have bought them. She isn't acting it there; they've bought no end of other unnecessary stuff. Parmesan, wine vinegar, three different kinds of bread. It must have cost a fortune. When they arrived back and got everybody outside helping unload the dozens of carriers from the boot, he and Robbie gave each other a look over the top of the car, the meaning of which was clear enough. How long do they think they're staying? They then proceeded to organize the putting away of the messages, cheerily deciding what was to go where, chucking out whatever dregs or no-good-enoughs were already on the shelves, as if by buying in all this better class of groceries, the kitchen was now theirs to do with as they wished.

The news is on. They sit watching and eating in quiet. It is the fifth night now Robbie and Jenna have brought through the chairs from the kitchen so they can all be in here, and they are in the habit already of keeping to the same seats. Alan and Lynn take the settee and, opposite, Mick sits between Robbie and his wife, the three of them sat close together like a row of naughty schoolweans sent to the headmaster's office. Craig is over in the armchair by the window, the head down, concentrating on his plate.

'It's some place now, the shopping centre at Braehead,' says Alan, setting his empty plate on the carpet in front of him. 'All new stores since we were last down there.'

The three of them look up and agree.

'I suppose it will be,' Mick says. 'I never go.'

'It's a great M&S,' says Lynn. 'Two levels, and a decent café. We stopped in for a sandwich when we'd done. And there's a dry ski slope down there now, I couldn't believe it. You should go over there and take a look, Mick.'

The weather comes on. It has been record temperatures for August, the guy says, and September is going to continue the same. Mick minds the time Cathy went down to the M&S, and what she'd thought about it, coming home with a single carrier of potatoes and mince. She wasn't impressed. It's too bloody expensive, was the verdict.

'You've seen the new apartments at Glasgow Harbour as well, have you?' Robbie says after a while, looking at Lynn.

'Yes. You pointed them out, didn't you, Alan? Very modern. About time they made more use out of all those dead areas along the river.'

'You think?' Robbie says, putting in a mouthful of Bolognese.

'I do,' Jenna breaks in, likely sensing Robbie's mood. 'Better developing than leaving it a wasteland.'

'There you are, then, Da. You should get one. You could have a wee balcony to sit on and look out over the water.'

Jenna gives Robbie a look, which because they are sat so close is right in Mick's face.

'There's no point leaving it to decay like it has been. Those cranes, and the berths all crumbling. It's not safe, for one thing. You're just being a mule, Robbie, you know it.'

He is feeling uncomfortable, these two starting to argue around him. He gets off his seat. Plus he needs to go up and check how much is in his wallet, to give toward the messages. As he leaves, he starts picking up the empty plates from the floor. Jenna is immediately helping him, reaching down for the Highlanders' plates before he has the chance. Maybe it isn't on purpose, but you never know. She's sensitive to things, Jenna; she knows the score.

In the kitchen they stack the plates by the sink. They're about to turn and go out when she presses her hand gently on top of his on the counter.

'You're pretty quiet today, Mick. How are you?'

'Coping on, I suppose.'

She smiles. 'It can't be easy, not when there's' – she raises the eyebrows a little – 'a houseful.'

He feels awkward, their hands touching there like that. Guilty, somehow, daft as it is.

'You shouldn't feel afraid to talk to these boys, you know. Even Craig. He's grieving, that's why he's being like he is.'

He tries to smile. She's a good girl, Jenna. Cathy was aye fond of her. She's down the line, is what it is. Honest. She's like Robbie that way, only less of the argle-bargle tendencies.

'It isnae that simple. He blames me.'

'He shouldn't. He's being selfish.'

'Aye, well. Maybe.' He looks away down the corridor. 'He keeps it inside himself. It was his maw he talked to.'

'Bulldust. You're here. And Robbie. He can talk to you.'

She takes her hand away.

'Come on,' she says, 'let's see how the party's going.'

'Okay. I'll be through in a moment, I'm going the toilet just.'

He goes upstairs to the bedroom. A ten-pound note, plus a bit of smash, it's all he's got on his tail. He can't offer that. If he gets up early again in the morning, maybe, he can nick out to the cash machine before any the rest of them are up. See what's in the account, then give Alan his share when he gets back. He'll tell him later the night that's what he's doing.

It's no exactly cheery, the mood in the living room. They're all sat there in the same positions, the television noisily on in the corner. It's like walking into a hospital waiting room, a bunch of edgy strangers pretending they're interested in the telly adverts – see maybe what he should do is bring in some old magazines for them to have a rummle through, distract themselves with the horoscopes and out-of-date TV listings.

He takes his seat. Looks around the room. Jesus. How long is this going to go on?

Jenna speaks. 'When are you back at the garage, Craig?'

They all turn to look at him. He keeps his eyes on the television.

'Don't know yet. Couple days. Depends how much is booked in.'

'Will you stay here or go back to your flat?'

'Go back. Too far to travel in from here.'

She doesn't push him. That's clear enough all he's going to say on the subject, and the room is silent again as they get back to their television watching. A quiz show. Two families in Englandshire competing one against the other for the incredible cash prize. A bald proud uncle with the spotlight on him now, chosen as the family expert on geography matters. A bit of patter with the show host as the countdown appears in the corner of the screen. Are you feeling confident? he gets asked. He is. It's his favourite category on the *Trivial Pursuits* at Christmas. Wee smiles along the family row.

It is the television that has become the centre of their movements. Up until yesterday it was Cathy. Her bed on the ward, when it had just been Robbie and Jenna here in the house, and then when she went, the arrival of the Highlanders and all the funeral arrangements to be sorted: undertakers, cemetery, wake spread; GP, register office, council. Now that it's all finished though, there's nothing for them to do but stick the TV on. Fact is, if it was to stop working they would be royally fucked. Or go home, maybe. He gives a keek over at Craig. He's sat with the arms folded, no expression, just staring. Don't come near me, is what he's saying. Don't come near me or I'll stiffen ye. He needs to get a moment to speak to him, Jenna is right about that. He'll be away without a word otherwise and then Christ knows what happens after that. Silence, probably.

He has brought it on himself but, he knows it fine well. No like he's made such a big effort to talk to the boy; ever, actually. All they years of sitting in the living room when Craig's come round to visit, leaving him and his maw to have their patter in the kitchen. It adds up sooner than you'd think, all that time. You start no to see that she's the one holding it together, and that without her, what kind of a relationship is there between you? Plus as well the boy as good as thinks that he killed her, which could prove a wee conversational stumbling block.

Alan gets up, asking if anybody is wanting anything from the kitchen. He goes out the room, quietly shutting the door behind him. In a moment – during which the bald uncle gets the spotlight took off him having pure disgraced himself as the family expert on geography matters – Mick follows him. He steps in the lobby just as Lynn is reminding everybody that she had known two of the answers.

Alan is bent inside the fridge. Mick comes in the room and he glances up at him as he pulls out a bottle of wine and sticks it on the counter.

'Would you like a glass, Mick?'

'I'm okay, thanks. No much of a wine drinker.' He stays by the counter, shuffling the great dump of post into more of a tidy pile.

Alan fetches himself a glass from the cupboard, pulls open a drawer for the corkscrew and gets opening his wine. Mick loiters over in the corner. He feels like a bloody houseguest. Alan takes a sip of wine and puts the bottle back in the fridge.

'You get to many Rangers games these days, Mick?'

'No much. Cathy being ill, it's –'

'No, sorry, I don't imagine you have.'

He has another drink of his wine. Mick fingers the envelopes. In truth, it's almost ten years, after Robbie left, since he was going to the games. And as well the season ticket increases. He slots the post in by the mini television. That's another thing will need seeing to before long. Brown envelopes. Some of these are from the same senders. Council. Housing Association. Her name is still on most of them. What happens about that, well? Is it the register office that wires it to all the relevant parties? Your computer tells my computer that such and such is to be wiped from the account. See the way it is with these bastards though, you more likely have to tell them yourself. Ten minutes waiting on the line to tell some poor bored hen in a call centre in East Kilbride that you want to advise a change in circumstances: I'm just ringing up to inform ye that my wife's died. Duly noted, Mr Little, I'll log it in the system for you.

Alan is staring away into the dark outside the window, drinking his wine. Then he turns round to him.

'How's work these days?'

There's a genuine unexpected topic of conversation between the two of them.

'It's a while since I've been driving, actually.'

'When do you think you might go back?'

'Well, I don't know. Soon enough. They said take as long as I want.'

'That's good of them.'

'Well. See they're no too busy.'

He should have said about the money earlier. Quick and simple.

'You know, Mick, you mustn't think that Cathy's family aren't here for you. They are. It's been hard for everybody.'

'I'm sure it has.'

'It's a really tough blow.' He makes it sound like a post office closure. 'You know any time you want to come up and stay at ours you're more than welcome. Have some dinner. Go out on the boat.'

'Right, thanks.'

Alan is stroking the stem of his wine glass. He turns again to look out at the small crap garden.

'Look, all this shopping,' Mick begins. 'Will ye let me give you something for it?'

Alan turns toward him. 'No, Mick, you don't need to.'

'No, I will. I won't have us not paying our way.' He glances up the corridor to the living room door, as though he's been sent to represent the others, the family shop steward.

'I won't take it. It came to a lot, anyway. I wouldn't want you to.'

'Wait here a moment just, will ye?' He leaves Alan fingering his wine glass while he goes from the room.

When he returns, Alan is stood where he was.

'Here.' He holds out the crumpled tenner. 'I'm going the cash machine in the morning, but here's this for now.'

The brother-in-law looks at the note a moment. 'Okay, then, Mick.' With a slow movement, he takes it from him. 'Thank you.'

He puts his glass down on the side and takes his wallet out the trouser pocket. As he flips it open, slipping the note in the back, there's an identity card, the top of his head poking out of one of the slots. A company card. How's he still carrying one of those? He's retired more than five years now. They must have kept him on, well – a consultant or something. An adviser. What I advise you is this: we've no enough orders for new ships and the yard isn't making enough profit, so get out the dunny money packets and lay the buggers off.

He is picking up his glass, and walks by Mick to the door. 'There's beers in the fridge if you want one,' he says over the shoulder.

Mick watches him away, the cards down the corridor flapping in the draught as his great back moves past them.

He stays in the kitchen a while, staring down toward the lobby. Then he opens the fridge and gets out a can. He drinks half of it in a single drain. Puts it down and wipes his lips.

Wanker.

3

It is hot and he can't sleep. The alarm clock across the way getting on for three o'clock. It's been pure stifling like this the last few nights and by now the heat is gathered in the upstairs rooms, no wind to blow it out. Earlier, Robbie and Jenna had went for a bit of air before bed, and came back saying it's near as muggy outside as it is in. Then Craig went out too, on his own, as he'd done the other nights. To the pub; you could smell it on him when he got back in. Mick had waited up after the others were away to their beds, but Craig was later back than usual, and in the end he decided it felt the wrong moment and he gave it a swerve.

He gets up and opens the other window. No difference. He leaves it open anyway and climbs back in the bed. She wouldn't've let him have it open. Breeze or no breeze. She hated a chill that much, grumbling on next to him with the covers pulled up to her chin, cauled tight around her. A soft familiar lump there in the bed. He stares at the alarm clock, waiting for the minute to switch over. This room, it's no like the other rooms. She has a say here still: the mirror with its collection of receipts and holiday competition cuttings wedged in the frame; the clutter of magazines by the wall; the electric heater on the other side of the bed with its broken outer bars.

He gets up again and goes out the room, needing the toilet. Afterwards, he goes down into the kitchen, where he turns the mini television on quiet, sits down at the table. Another quiz show. A young girl hosting it. She's got on this lunatic smile as she picks up the phone, waiting for the caller to guess the blank. The first word is *Iron*. The guy on the line seems pretty sure he's got it. '*Statue*,' he says. The girl turns to look at the giant screen behind her in mock excitement. 'Let's see if it's there . . . No!' She slaps her thigh. 'Not this time, Terry.'

It's fair obvious the people ringing up to do this at half three in the morning are either blootered or they're no the full ticket. The next one, a shrill woman called Christie, could be either way. 'Is it *board*?' she asks. It isn't. 'Unlucky, Christie. Better luck next time.' There is what looks like a flicker of desperation on the girl's face. I hope they pay ye well for this, hen. He turns it off and gets up to go back to bed.

3.54. The alarm clock, that's her as well. She'd got it years ago with his saved-up petrol coupons from the cab. He knocked it on the floor a couple of days ago when he was tidying up the things on her table, and the plug came out. Setting the time and date again proved a complete impossibility – he's never all these years figured out how the thing works – and so for the past two nights the alarm has come on at some point in the early hours. Both times, it took him bloody ages working out which button shuts it up, and then he spent what was left of last night finally fixing it out: time, date, bastard thing. No that he was that put out, in truth. He was awake anyway.

He moves himself over the other side of the bed. He may as well have stayed put in the kitchen. Given a call in to the show. *Iron Age. Iron Lady.* A look of pure relief on the girl that she's no the only sane person up the night. Down there in the kitchen, the living room too, the things are things just, she isn't present in them. Hard to say how that is when it's her that bought most of it but that's how it feels, unlike up here in this room. He's surrounded by her here, but he isn't a part of it himself. It is strange, the other side of the bed. Unknown lumps and bumps of wiring poking up at the mattress. He's got a queer awareness of what it would have felt like for her, on her side. He lies a while longer, staring at the alarm clock, until, at the back of five, he gets out of bed and lays down on the floor next to it, pulling the covers down over him.

There is a toilet roll under the bed. A pair of broken sunglasses. He should give a clean under there, he gets thinking as finally he starts to drift off. Add that to the list.

4

A cemetery worker is busy sweeping along a flagstone path, collecting up the dirt into a wheelbarrow. He has seen the man there by his wife's grave each of the last few days: he comes in the morning and stands there a long time, staring down at the ground. Obvious that he's having a hard time of it, and so he makes sure to keep his distance now as he gets about clearing the path and tidying the area around a plot he's to measure and mark later the morning.

He has seen the rest of the family here as well. They come all at different times; even before the service, he knows from his manager that there'd been some difficulties with the arrangements. A guy that it seems is the brother of the deceased comes with his wife, and they stay a short time rearranging the flowers; the son with the queer accent, he gets here after lunch and stays holding his partner's hand; and then the older son comes after the others have gone. He's always the one that stays the longest. Yesterday, he was sat on the grass next to the grave almost the whole afternoon, getting a book out at one point and just staying there reading.

He pushes the wheelbarrow off down the lawn to the store room, where he puts it away with the broom and the shovel. He fills a bucket with water and takes a stiff brush, a pair of black rubber gloves and a container of solvent from a shelf, then he goes out of the store and down toward the road. The cemetery wall has been defaced again – K.A.H., it reads, sprayed in large black lettering over the concrete – and he kneels down on the pavement to get scrubbing at it with the thick creamy solvent. From where he is, he can just about see the grey head of the man, grieving beside his wife's grave. Poor guy. There had been kind of an awkward atmosphere after the service, and it's a fair guess the family relationship's no the best. Always politics somewhere. He was in the yards, this one, according to his manager. That whole length of path is lined with the names of yardmen, copped their whack before their time.

21

A whole shop floor under that lawn, he'd heard the registrar say a while back, and it would be true enough, except that so many of them are the wives and weans. He keeps on scouring the wall a few more minutes – it doesn't get rid of it, but it's the best he can do, the solvent and then the sun beating down on it between now and when it gets painted over at the end of the summer. When he's done, he picks up the bucket and container and walks back through the cemetery, passing the man, who is stood now by the black iron palings on the other side of the grave, gazing down.

Mick is reading the tags on the flower bouquets. There's a new big bunch from the Highlanders that they must have got in the Marks and Spencer. A smaller one from Pete and Mary. He puts the tags back as they were, and gets ready to leave. The first few times he's come here, he's stayed almost an hour, looking down at the mound of not yet sunken earth. He tries to imagine her. It's no easy but. Each time, he ends up standing there just, trying to feel that she's there, trying to see her face, but it's no happening, is the truth – he may as well be stood staring at a car engine for all the closeness he's getting.

Maybe when the headstone is up, it will feel different. Although even that hadn't been without its difficulties. It was him that gave the inscription for it; Alan had paid. The only thing they'd went halves on was the coffin. When they were in the funeral director's, Mick had called for a modest and simple box, saying that it was what she would have wanted, although of course he knew fine well that if she had any say in it she would have gone for the most expensive one in the shop. He turns to leave, looking down at the space next to her as he moves off, lush and well tended, the stalks of the flower bunches resting down over it, like she's saving a seat for him on the bus.

The Highlanders are in the kitchen when he gets back, one of them carefully monitoring the grill and the other holding a saucepan.

'Craig about?' he asks, his head through the doorway. Sausage and beans, it looks like.

'In the bathroom, I think,' says Lynn. 'You ready for some breakfast?'

'Aye, thanks,' he says, eyeing the sausages as she gets turning them over. 'I'll be through in a minute.'

He goes up and waits just inside the bedroom, hoping to catch Craig as he comes past. But when the bathroom door clicks and he makes his move, it is Robbie that is stepping out. They stop there a moment on the stairhead.

'Been the grave?'

'Aye, I'm just back.'

'You okay?'

'I'm fine, Rob, thanks.'

In the kitchen, he and Robbie get themselves a plate of breakfast from the dishes on the table and go through to the living room, where the others are already eating.

Robbie and Jenna have booked their flights, they say. Monday morning. There's a stop-off in Hong Kong, and they could've arranged to stay a night, but they're wanting to get back to the baby. At the mention of this, Lynn gets telling the story of their own trip to India a couple of years ago: how the flight was a nightmare and the locals pack into the trains like pilchards, and there's cows in the road but if you hire a driver he won't even pamp the horn at them. Mick's not much interested in another of Lynn's stories; he's thinking instead how he's going to manage taking Craig aside. His best bet, he knows, is when the house is quieter, that's obvious enough, while the Highlanders are off on one of their visits to the Botanic Gardens or the Tenement House. He'll have to wait just, bide his time. Chin him before he goes visiting the grave.

But the Highlanders have for some reason decided against an excursion. They stay in the house fussing on all morning, and it means the right moment doesn't come; and so by early afternoon, when Robbie and Jenna return from the grave, Craig is out the door. Like the other days, he's away a long while, not getting in until the back of six, when the house is busy and the Highlanders are preparing food again. It isn't until after tea and the evening of television watching, when Craig is about to get up and leave, that he has an opportunity.

Craig is after excusing himself from the room, away to the lobby to put on his jacket. Mick gets off his seat and follows him.

He is by the front door, the jacket on, searching his pockets.

'I might come join ye for a nightcap, if that's alright,' Mick says, reaching for his own brown jacket off the hook. He can feel the eyes looking at him.

'Aye, if ye want.'

They keep on quick along the pavement. The blue light of televisions flickering through windows as they go down the street; heads, lager cans, weans lying on their fronts. Craig is walking at a fair crack. They stay side by side, and he has a job keeping up.

'Ye go the Empress, is it?'

'Usually. It's quiet in there.'

'Aye, well, nothing changes, eh?' He falls back to let Craig pass a lamppost, and hurries on after. 'There many in there ye know?'

'No really. Only Desmond.'

He chuckles. 'See that's what I mean. Nothing changes.'

Desmond. A fine familiar and reassuring figure. Comb-over wrinkling under the gantry lights; the big potato hands lining up whisky tumblers along the drip trays to catch each last drop from the lager taps. He should thank him again for the wake, he gets thinking, as they turn onto the high street. It's busy the night, smokers stood outside the Brazier and a queue out the door of the chip shop. Rangers were away the day but there's still plenty of Blue-noses about the place. The two of them march on through. Keen to get on and be sat down with a drink.

It's not Des behind the bar though. There's a woman he doesn't recognize as he goes up for their drinks and Craig sits down at a table in the corner. The tumblers are there on the drip trays though, so he's about somewhere. Probably in the back, reading his detective novels. Glass of Grouse. Fag plugged in the ashtray. Disturb me at your peril, hen, disturb me at your fucking peril.

She holds the glass under the tap and allows the froth to slurp over the rim, slowly pooling in the tumbler underneath. Mick turns to keek over at Craig, where he is sat by the window staring up at the football highlights. Why is it they're here, again? He's no too sure any more. What was he expecting – a nice wee chat? A pure certainty that isn't going to happen, and yet here they are; he's pushed himself on the boy to come out for a drink but now they're here he knows fine well it can only end in a fight. What choice has

24

he got but? Nay choice. They need to have some kind of a conversation, whatever else happens. It isn't his fault the boy sits there like a cauldron and you can't get near him. Not totally his fault, anyway, no the full share.

He pays for the drinks. As he picks them up off the counter he catches sight, through the bar, of a recognizable shape sat in the parlour, hunched over a Guinness.

'Pat,' he calls through. No response, so Mick puts the pints down a moment to go round and say a quick hello.

'Pat.'

He looks up.

'Mick. How ye getting on?'

'Fine. Keeping a lid on it, ye know.'

Pat looks through to the main bar, past the two lagers sat on the far counter. 'Ye have the family with you, eh?'

'I do. All of them.'

'It was Tuesday, they said.'

'It was, aye.'

Pat nods. 'Ye have my condolences, Mick.'

With that, he turns back to his drink, and the matter is at a close. Condolences dispensed. They say goodbye.

Round the other side, Mick picks up the lagers and regards Pat a moment sipping his Guinness. He's certain a worse state than whenever last he saw him. The nose is badly gone the now, sore and swollen, delicately fractured with blood vessels. What do you expect? The guy's been coming in here for decades. He's in with the bricks. He was sat right there almost thirty years ago when him and Cathy moved back from Australia, his grumbling presence even then moiled into the sight and smell of the place, as crucial a part of it as the framed battleships along the walls or the great dark stain on the ceiling. There was a brief period just, after the smoking ban came in, when he stopped coming. Desmond had told him, the big hands braced on the counter, that he'd no choice but towing the line. He wasn't risking the fine. Pat had simply got up off his stool and walked out. 'That's fine, well. I will take my custom elsewhere.' And he'd went round the bar and left, simple as that, closing the door quietly behind him. That's me, pal. I'm off. Ye have my condolences. He was back within the month though. Climbed onto his seat at the bar and ordered his Guinness as if nothing had ever happened. No word was spoke again about the incident, and you'd never know that Pat gave it another thought except that now, whenever he goes for a smoke outside, he lights up his fag as he's walking through the bar, and takes that first draw while he's still in the lobby, getting open the door.

'Here we are, son.' Mick places the pints on the small table and sits in opposite.

'Cheers.' Craig takes a drink of his lager and looks back up at the television. Mick joins his gaze. Hibs and Aberdeen. No the most compelling TV viewing. The commentator is the main noise in the room, which is pretty empty. A few tables across there is a man silently out with his wife; by the toilets, the occasional whine and clobber of the fruit machine, a young lad going away at it.

'The Rangers game been on yet?' Mick asks.

'No yet. They won though.'

Through the bar, past Pat, there's two old boys on the faded red wall seat that goes around the parlour, pattering away together. He takes a long sup, observing Craig over the top of his glass.

'When did ye last get down?'

'Eh?'

'I say when was it ye last got down?'

'How ye mean? Down where?'

'Ibrox.'

'Oh, right. Years ago. With you, probably.'

'Christ, long time ago, that. Motherwell, was it, two–nil? I can mind that, I think.'

'It was Hearts.'

'Aw, aye, that's right, it was.'

They go quiet again. Get watching the football. The Celtic match comes on and the man and his wife turn to have a look at the screen. They've played at home and he doesn't recognize who they're against, but whoever it is, it looks like Celtic have cuffed them. Is this what he's been doing? he thinks with sudden pity. Sat here watching this keech on his own. Is it that bad he'd rather this than stay in the house? Obviously it is. What can he do about it but?

There's nothing he can say that's going to put everything right, no now, it's too built up, and the boy's obvious no in the mood to listen either so anything he says is just going to dig him up the worse. Being honest, the best thing is for him to get back across town to his flat. Go back to work. See his mates. He's no doing himself any good maundering away here, and the truth is, say what you want about it, but it will be a relief tomorrow when he's gone. There. He admits it. The bastard father, spilling the beans. Celtic's match is still on – three–nil, four–nil, more maybe – but Mick's gaze drops away from the screen and he starts staring at the wall underneath the television mount, at the brown pitted wallpaper like moulding orange peel, and at the pictures hanging unevenly in rows. Ships and footballers, mixed together: the *Bloodhound*, HMS *Valiant*, Davie Meiklejohn, HMS *Indomitable*, Willie Johnston, RMS *Empress of Japan*, Alan 'The Wee Society Man' Morton. Clydebuilt, each every one, crafted and revered all down the water, talked about over people's teatimes, sold off to England. Some of the players probably worked on these ships. They probably did; that's how it was. They would have served their apprenticeships on the yards, black squad, up early for a day's work, and then away for a quick shower and a bite to eat and they'd be down the training pitches. There was one guy he'd went to school with, Andy Loy, was in the juniors at Rangers: a great young player, fast, skilful, but he didn't make the cut. Close, but no quite. He'd stayed on at John Brown's instead, and become the yard's ratcatcher. A terrible job in truth but the daftie bugger had loved it. This wee stinking hut that he'd worked out of – the shelves piled with poisons and explosives and rusted weaponry – but the swarming hordes all about the place never getting any less because Andy wasn't going to risk losing his job so he only ever killed the male ones.

The fruit machine is ringing and a spew of coins clatters into the collect tray. The lad has struck it lucky. You can see by his face how pleased he is, the money falling out from the machine for quite a long while. Good for you, pal. Mick gives him a grin as he comes past on his way to the bar with the coins cupped in his hands, a wee smile from Craig too, glancing down a moment from the television. It's his own face, if anything, not his mother's. They've similar features. It gets more noticeable the older he is. Even a few grey hairs showing already. That'll be another thing he can hold against him.

He stays looking at the boy for a moment before turning back to the wall. Rats. That was one thing that never changed. As a wean, his da would take him into the yard sometimes when a ship was due for its trials, and they'd stand together in a big crowd of boys and yardmen as the ship got fumigated, waiting for the moment when hundreds of rats started pouring down the mooring ropes, and then the popcorn-popping sound as everyone got batting them with their shovels.

Desmond is walking over.

He stands over the table, a great bear blocking out the television.

'Mick. It's good to see you.'

'And yourself, Desmond. How's it going?'

'No bad, aye, no bad. Quiet, like, but what can ye do, eh?' He claps a giant hand onto Craig's shoulder. 'Robbie still here as well, is he?'

'He is. And the Highlanders. They're off the morrow but, any luck.'

'Aye, well, good of them to stay this long, I suppose. Alan been putting the mix in?'

'No, he's been fine, to be fair. Lynn's been cooking for us all, so there's no complaints really. Look, Des, I wanted to say thanks again for the other day. It –'

'Aw, Mick, serious, it's no a problem. Ye're very welcome. And it's no like I'm mobbed with custom, know?' He looks round toward the bar. 'I'm sure Pat coped with himself for a few hours.' He chuckles, taking the hand off Craig's shoulder, and looks down at the table. 'Another drink, boys?'

Craig shakes his head.

'No, we're alright, thanks,' Mick says.

'Okay, well, yous two take care. I'd best go see what state this bar's in.'

His massive arse is moving away to the bar. They look up to the television as the Rangers game comes on. There's an early goal. He doesn't recognize the scorer. Maybe he should try and persuade Craig to stay for another drink. Force something out of him, at least. How's he getting on up in Yoker, for one thing; is the job working out? Apart from the bits and pieces that Robbie's told him, he honestly wouldn't know. Does he have a girlfriend even? The thought of asking him something like that. Excuse me, son, but I was wondering just if ye're seeing anybody the now, and how does she get on with these thundery mood swings of yours? Probably he wouldn't be like that with her though. See she would understand him; she would make time and listen to him.

Desmond is talking to the new barmaid, showing her something at the till. After a moment they move along the bar and he pulls down a couple of whisky bottles from the gantry, unscrews the pourer off the fuller one and starts marrying them together, shaking out the last few drops from the empty. Then back onto the rack. He leaves her to get doing the rest of the bottles while he goes over by the till, carefully patting the comb-over, and observes her. The thought occurs to him then, minding the hand on Craig's shoulder, that possibly Desmond knows more what's going on with him than he does. If this is his hideout, where he comes to get away from the house, from him, he might well have talked a little to Des. Even if no how he's feeling, then maybe at least some of the other stuff, like how's his flat and his job, and is his boss a bastard and all that type of thing.

'I'm off home, Da.'

Craig stands up, pulling his jacket on.

'Okay, son, I'll come with ye.'

It is dark, walking back. The streetlamps are on, and there aren't as many people about as earlier, though there's still a queue in the chip shop. They turn off the high street, through an alleyway, and past a group of bevvied-up young lads playing football in the dim light of a back court. It could have gone worse, he tells himself. They got through it without any explosions, at least. That's something. Give it time, is the best thing. Let him be alone with himself for a while, no having to deal with people in his face the whole day. He's a solitary kind of a person, anyway, so he'll figure himself out if he's left to it. They come past the bus stop at the end of the road and as they get near the house he can see the lights are off downstairs, so Robbie and Jenna must be away to bed.

Even as he opens the front door, it doesn't really hit him that she isn't going to be there. There's no thudding realization whacking him over the head or anything like that, it's more a feeling like she's out, like it's bingo night or something. He goes into the kitchen and gets himself a glass of water while Craig goes up to the bathroom. The Highlanders have tidied away all the cans and the bottles into separate carriers, he notices. He drinks his water and waits until he can hear Craig coming down the stair. They pass in the corridor.

'Night,' Craig says, going into the living room.

'Night, son. See you in the morning.'

He hasn't slept in the bed any of these last nights. All the bedding is now pulled onto the floor, against the wall, with Robbie's old camping mat underneath for him to lie on. He's been sleeping better there. No perfect, but it's better. It still takes a few hours each night, trying to block out the sound of Fred fucking Flintstone through the wall, until he gets drifting off. And when he does, he sleeps in short, deep spurts, waking often, and usually from the most pure vivid dreams. She is there in most of these, even if it's just for a walk-on: crossing the road as he's waiting in a car stopped at the lights, or sat near to him at the bus stop eating a sausage roll. More often though, the dreams are about her, or the two of them together. He had one, she was in the kitchen getting tea ready, some keech on the mini TV in the background, and she's chatting away to herself as he comes in and gets himself a beer out the fridge. Then when she sees him she starts straight away apologizing, saying she's no had time to fix out a proper tea and so it's ham and eggs and he's genuine bemused, laughing, because what's wrong with ham and eggs – that's a great bloody tea.

It is colder the night and he's got the windows closed. Still the odd noise from outside: a front door shutting; a car speeding toward the river. He pulls the covers in close over him, and starts to feel quite snug there on the floor, and maybe it's the beer he drank but it isn't long before he has started gradually, comfortably, to drop off.

He is in the bed and she's lying next to him, facing away, snoring. He can't sleep, it's that loud. The noise increases steadily to a peak, and stops with a jolt; a moment of peace and silence as she lies there breathing heavily, and then it begins again. He props himself up on his elbow and looks over at her. The flesh of her neck bunched against her chin. He gives her a shunt with his elbow and lies quickly down again. Silence. A few moments' respite, and then it gets up again. He gives another nudge and she grunts to a stop. He closes his eyes and pretends he's asleep. She mumbles some nonsense a few seconds and goes quiet. After a while he feels himself starting to fall to sleep, the eyes slowly closing, but then she's at it again. He gives a real shunt this time, and turns quick over onto his other side. There is a chuckle. 'I know what ye're up to. Pack it in, eh.' He kids on he's asleep, but he can't keep it up and soon he's chuckling too.

He turns over toward her, but she's gone – he sees her suddenly over by the wardrobe, getting dressed. 'Come on, you, get a move on. They'll be closing soon.' He gets up and changes and they go down the staircase, but when they get to the bottom they are on the lower deck of a bus, taking a seat at the back over the engine, because she is cold. She keeps chuffing her hands together to warm them up. They are about to get off, and the driver calls to them to come over. When they get to the glass side of the cab he looks in and it is the barmaid from the Empress. She's got all these photos stuck up around the cab. This one of her weans, two wee girls, playing in a paddling pool. She looks annoyed about something. 'Go on, get off, then,' she says, so they do and they step out into the car park of the Co. He fetches a trolley and they go inside, where it's very busy, and hard to move around. He jostles the trolley up an aisle, with the wife in beside him reeling off a list of things they are needing: carrots, tatties, bog roll, flowers. She sends him off to the freezers for a chicken, but when he's got it he can't find her again, the place is too hoaching with shoppers. He tries going down the central aisle to look both sides and he is up and down twice before he sees her – she's at the checkout, sat in a booth. When he gets on the approach he can see that she's wearing a blue shirt and a Co badge with her name on it. He gets unloading the trolley and she passes each of the items over the scanner, her head down. He notices then that she is greeting. 'What is it, hen?' he says, but she doesn't answer, she keeps scanning the shopping. 'It's okay,' and he tries to take her hand as she scans the bog roll. 'We can go now,' he says. He can't see her face but he knows she's smiling, and she stands up to leave the booth, but the door is locked and it won't open. She shakes it, and he gets helping her but it won't budge and he can hear her sobbing again. 'Climb over it, hen. Come on, try, will ye? We can go now, look, I've got all the shopping – I got the tatties, see?'

He's said these last words out loud, he realizes, sitting up from the mat with a plaster-peeling sound. He stays a moment with his arms folded on top of his knees, getting his bearings, looking out the window to get a fix on what is real. The brainbox in a muddle still. He stares out as, slowly, it clears. There's something of a moon the night. You can see it above the dark blocks of the multis. Five or six black shapes with only a few windows lit, and the yellow spines of the stairwell lights – one of them flickering, up near the top.

5

Craig is the first to leave. His bag is packed up and ready by the door when the rest of them have finished their breakfast.

'What time will you start work tomorrow?' Lynn asks him as they gather in the lobby, watching him put on his jacket.

'I'm in early. I'll talk with my boss and see what's what.'

He gives her a stiff hug, and the rest of them line up along the corridor to see him off.

'Don't be a stranger, now,' Alan says to him. The kind of thing you say to people who are strangers.

'Okay,' Craig replies, and it is actually rare comic – the look on his face – it's that obvious he'd rather top himself. Mick looks over at Robbie, wondering if he's thought the same. Robbie's looking pretty serious but. He's next up, and he gives his brother a tight squeeze. There's a look between them that's hard to read. Understanding, maybe. Disagreement.

When it gets his turn it is in the end quite easy. With all the rest of them stood watching there's no question of a wee private chat, so they stick to the formalities just. A brief hold. A pat on the back.

'Come over for your tea sometime soon, eh?'

'Okay, I will.'

And he's away. Off to wait at the bus stop and get moving across town.

The Highlanders are next. A drawn-out carry-on of hugs and promises shortly after *Cash in the Attic*. Poor Lynn hardly able to bring herself to get leaving, she's that torn up about it.

They decide the three of them to go for a walk in the afternoon. The sun's come out again after the cloudy spell of the last couple of days, and they go up the park for a bit of a wander. It's enjoyable. Being able to relax and have a bit of patter finally, and no be wary the whole time of treading on eggshells. It's a shame there's only this day left. Robbie and Jenna's flight goes early in the morning. They've got their taxi to the airport booked already, and Jenna has tidied up their stuff from the living room. For now, walking through the middle of the park, past a fringe of small planted flowers, Jenna is asking him what his plans are for the next couple of days, after they've gone. He'll give a call into work, he says, see when they need him. Get the house cleaned up. Finish off the parmesan. He grins, but the pair of them have got their concerned faces on. Obvious enough what they're thinking: how will he get on, on his own? Will he manage? Will he hit the drink?

'How was it last night, with Craig?' Robbie asks.

'Yeh, it was fine.'

'Really? The two of you get to talk?'

'Aye, well, kind of. Mean, it isnae easy. But there was no bust-up at least. How, has he said anything to you?'

'No. Not much, anyway.' They slow up a moment as a young boy chases across the path after a football. 'See I was just wondering last night if he might talk to you about compensation and that.'

'No, he didnae. He has to you, then?'

'Not directly. I know it's on his mind though. He brought it up the other day, how more cases are being brought, and there's been some big victories and that. There was one last month, apparently, don't know if you saw, a hundred and fifty grand, he says.'

'It's no a victory, Robbie.'

'I know, Christ. That's not how Craig sees it either, you know. He's angry, Da. He's just angry. He needs to blame somebody. And they're as good as anybody, aren't they – the employers, the insurance companies – he's right about that, isn't he?'

They come past a battered play area with a swing and a mangled see-saw. The seat on the swing is come unfixed from the chain on one side, and juts down like a broken bone.

'Da?'

'I don't know, Rob. I don't know what I think.' He looks ahead up the path. 'You agree with him, then? You think we should put in a claim?'

'I'm not sure. It's your decision, Da.' He glances across at Jenna.

'We're obviously not going to be around through it all, so it's not for me to say.'

'Of course it bloody is. She was your maw too. You've as much right as Craig or anybody else.'

Robbie goes quiet as they walk on. He notices, further on, Jenna take his hand as the path widens and they come toward the far side of the park.

'Now's no the time to be thinking about it, anyway,' Mick says after a while. 'Come on.' And they leave the park with the sun still going brightly over the tenements, starting back to the house.

They get a carry-out from the curry shop for their tea, a bit of cargo from the offie. Robbie insists paying for it. Says he's hardly put his hand in his pocket the whole while he's been here. Fine. It's no like you can argue with him anyway. They watch a film after they've eaten – a good one, Australian, as it happens, even though it's just what's on the television. It's about this guy who's a notorious hardcase, robs drug dealers and cuts their toes off kind of thing, but who doesn't let a long stretch in the clink stop him from keeping up with his psychie tendencies: stabbing, torturing, and then writing a book and becoming a celebrity – true story, apparently. Robbie and Jenna tell him the guy's well known over there as a writer and a lunatic. When the film's finished, they stay up and finish the beers. Chatting. No about anything much, just chatting. It's good; he enjoys their company. It is the back of midnight by the time they're done, so when their taxi comes at six the next morning to pick them up, the pair of them are a wee bit groggy-looking as he comes down the stair to say goodbye.

He gets a good long hug off them both.

'Like I said, Da, I'll come over again soon. That's a promise.'

'Ye don't have to promise me, Rob. I know the score. It's okay.'

After the taxi has left he comes back inside and carries upstairs the pile of bedding that Jenna has left neatly folded by the settee. When it's all put away he comes back down and makes himself a cup of tea.

He gets a window open in the living room. Let the place breathe a bit, lessen the aroma of farting sons. Poor Jenna, serious. She for one must be looking forward to being in her own bed again, that's a banker. Getting back to the baby. It's been a long time away for them, new parents that they are, and he's genuine grateful they stayed this long. Robbie might well say that he'll be over again soon but it's a daft promise to make, which is how he wasn't entertaining it, no even for a moment. Maybe if they leave it a while, then next time Damien might be old enough they can bring him too. Get him introduced. It's one of the things he's had a struggle with, Robbie, that his maw never met the baby. He knows that, because Jenna told him. Robbie didn't want to say anything about it himself because he thinks it's too close the knuckle and he doesn't want to make things any the harder for his father. Which is daft, obviously. It's something he wouldn't've minded talking to him about. But that's Robbie: always this sense – whether it's the Highlanders, or it's Craig, or it's the compensation – that he's trying to protect him. Keep things from getting any the worse. That he doesn't completely trust him to cope with things on his own, without him, without Cathy.

He goes into the kitchen and opens a drawer. From under magazines and cookbooks he takes out a card, then goes to sit down at the table and read again the letter that is tucked inside it.

Mick,

I am so sorry for your loss. I wouldn't for a moment tell you I know what you're going through because it's different for all of us, but I know nothing can prepare you for when it happens. And when it does you need to know your friends are there for you, like you and Cathy were for me when John went.

It's not my place to say it Mick but you can't blame yourself. We didn't know in those days. How could we? There wasn't all the studies like there are now. I know it's a difficult situation for you because of Alan being in the management and now's not the time for it either, but if you want I can tell you the people to go to if you're thinking about going down the justice and compensation route. Like I say, I know you probably don't want to think about any of this yet but they knew, Mick. Even back then. They should have done checks. For Christ's sake, John used to come home in his overalls white as a baker and I'd shout at him for getting the dust in my carpets. It's not about the money. It's about justice. If you want to talk then please do give me a call. I'm on the same number. God knows, it might do me good myself. Take your time.

All the best
Alice

After a moment, he slips the letter back inside the card and returns it to the drawer. The idea of it – justice – seems pure absurd. Alice is gone down that route and fair enough, that's her decision, but the thought of it – how many thousands have died and still you've to tear yourself inside out dragging through the courts before any of these bastards will admit for a moment it's their fault. And it's no even him dead. Him that played snowballs with the stuff and came home with it stored in the turn-ups of his trousers. Justice is a word for it maybe, getting the payout, but it doesn't feel sitting here like the right one, no the right one at all.

He goes back through and flicks the tellybox on, settles himself into the cushions, and it isn't long before he is away to sleep.

She is there in his dreams again. They are that real – that's what's hard to get the head round. The two of them are washing and drying up. They're eating chips. They're arguing in the garden. Short dreams that come and go but don't finish, carrying on one to the next but connected somehow, linked up, like a chain of islands each with their different goings on but the same backdrop all around, the same light, the same weather following through the dreams so that if in one of them the wind is blustering at her washing while she hangs it out, in the next she'll be there in the crowd at a ship launch with everybody holding on top of their hats.

The sun is on his face, and he spots the postie turning in through the gate. He gets sat up. The body feels heavy, solid. He listens to the footsteps on the concrete and the clank of the letterbox. He is awake, that's obvious enough, but he has this sense of being detached from things. As if all these goings on around him – the sunshine, Phillip Schofield grinning on the television, the post tummelling onto the mat – they are all part of some other life, one that he can see, but he's not involved in. Mental, really. But that's what it's like. And even trying to keep up with the Japanese and the French and the Germans. How not the brother-in-law? But he was shut away, wasn't he, the door snibbed closed, pouring whisky down the throats of shipowners and insurance men. We've upheld our responsibilities and don't think we haven't. We've put the signs up – telling about ventilation and masks and dust checks and all these things that were never bothered with and nobody ever thought to ask for because you couldn't read the bloody sign even, it was that covered in fucking dust.

He presses himself into the crack between the ground and the wall, trying to stop the wind getting a run on him as it races through. The whole of him is aching. Hardly a surprise. It's pure ancient, this camping mat, worn down almost to nothing and if it wasn't already then it will be soon, all this tossing and turning he's doing. Another gulp of whisky. And another. Liars. Fucking liars – see what about all they poor bastards up at the asbestos factory actually making the stuff, hadn't they been lied to worse than anyone? You'd see them coming out with it pasted wet over them from head to toe from hosing the machines down. Each holding a newspaper to stick under the bahookie when they sat on the bus, trying no to piss the driver off. They'd been told it was only dangerous when it was dry. So they took it home, and then what happened – what do ye think bloody happened? – it dried again, didn't it, but that was fine, far as the powers that be were concerned, that wasn't a danger. Fucking lies, all of it. They deserved everything that was coming to them. And if it was him dying, then maybe he would go down that route. Secure a future for Cathy. But it wasn't; it was him brought the stuff in the house. And he should have known. Even if no at first, way back, then he certain could have done later on, when there was the warnings and the newspaper reports and he could have seen through all these lies and no been so blind to it. He'd even worked with somebody who thought they'd took a bad back. Actually known somebody die who'd thought that at first, but then when it was Cathy in the doctor's he didn't think to say anything about it, he fucking forgot.

Could ye have put it out at any time, anything ye can mind? Well, the vacuuming, maybe. See I had a wee twinge doing under the kitchen table no long back. And that was that. Decided. She'd took a bad back. All ye can do is rest it up a few weeks and do nothing – let the man of the house get acquainted with the vacuum for a while, eh? They'd all had a chuckle at that. And he did do as well: vacuuming, cleaning, ironing, with her sat laughing at him the whole month until they went back in when she couldn't stop coughing.

He can't shut the thoughts out now. He presses his forehead hard against the wood, as if to fight against them, but it's no use, it doesn't help. And see if he did put a claim in then the reminders would be there the whole time – for months, years, however long it took – and even that is still ignoring the main thing: why should *he* get a windfall? Him that brought it into the house and handed her the overalls to wash and here's two hundred grand, pal, take it, it's yours – you deserve it.

10

The head is crawling. Stupit. He looks over at the bottle and not only has he wrecked his head, he's also wasted half the whisky rations. No very wise, but there you go, it's no the end of the world; which, in fact, isn't looking too bad this morning: the sun streaming in onto his legs through the small grubby window. He lies there awake a time, listening to the sound of things outside. Birds. A door closing. A distant radio. And all the while playing his toe around something soothingly cool and damp that it's probably no wise investigating what it is.

Anyway, up and at it. He goes to the kitchen, where he takes off his shirt and trousers and gives himself a wash from the sink. He dries himself with the one remaining teacloth, puts the clothes back on, and makes himself a pair of boiled eggs and a slice of toast for cutting into soldiers. Nothing like a boiled egg for a hangover. Except when he lops the heads off he finds he's done them too long and they are gone solid, so he scrapes them out with a teaspoon instead. He needs to go into work the day, get some shifts. It's unavoidable. The longer he leaves it the less they'll want him, and anyway he needs the money.

He stays sat in the kitchen a long time trying to force himself up. But he can't do it; he isn't ready. It feels too much – anyway he looks at it, it feels too much, even bloody getting there, christsake, even the prospect of that is bringing him out in a sweat. The morrow. He'll go the morrow. Rain or shine.

The nights are getting colder. He goes in the house and up the stair one afternoon for more blankets, a fresh shirt and trousers and a jumper, an action that proves a pure effort of will in itself even, just drumming up the balls to go into the bedroom. And the whisky is long finished too, which doesn't help matters.

After three stops, he starts to relax a little. Nobody is noticing him. They're on a different planet, these people, with their earphones plugged in, or just staring out the window. Even when Bertie the workshop mechanic gets on, it's fine, because he's stood in a spot near the back of the bus from where Bertie can't see him, two dozen armpits and raw razored faces in the way between. It's pure illogical but. He's going to have to see him soon enough, he knows. And Bertie's alright, anyway. He's a rare auld ticket in fact, always in there with a joke or a wee story to keep everybody amused. Mick watches him through the armpits. Even Bertie is away with the fairies this morning, it seems, dreaming up something or other, a funny tale to tell the drivers.

He lets Bertie get a way up the street ahead of him, and follows on behind. The stomach is something jittery getting when he turns onto the lane, but there's nobody about and so he goes straight in the office, a shabby small space set into one corner of the workshop, with a plywood divider on one side, and a computer desk and Lynsey in her headset on the other. She's typing something and doesn't notice him when he comes in. Her face concentrated on the screen, clabbered with make-up.

'Mick,' she says, looking up.

'Hello, Lynsey, how's it going?'

'Fine, Mick, fine.' She is uncomfortable seeing him, it is obvious enough. Doesn't know what to say. That makes two of them, well.

'I spoke to Malcolm. He said to come in.'

'Did he? He's no told me anything.' She looks at her screen a moment, then back at him. 'He's gone out just now, I don't know when he's due back. Will I give him a call on his mobile?'

'No, no, that's fine, Lynsey. I'll wait for him a while just, if that's okay?'

'Aye, if ye like.' She smiles, and he tightens up, ready for it, but then she says, 'There's Bertie about somewhere, and a couple of the drivers. Go have a wander. I'm sure they'd like to see you.'

He looks at the divider. The sound of an engine from in the shop.

'If it's alright I'll stay here for now, if I'm no disturbing you.'

'Naw, it's fine. Don't worry. Ye sure ye don't want me to give him a call but? See I don't know when he'll be back and he might be a while.'

'It's okay, thanks.'

There is a chair on the other side of the office, and he goes over to sit on it. He stays there a moment, looking around, noticing the gap beside the divider that looks into the shop. He gets up again, Lynsey glancing at him from her desk, and he walks over to a metal cabinet, on top of which is a paper. He stands reading it, or looking at it anyway. The corkboard on the wall beside him is pretty empty. Normally there would be a long list of accounts and pre-bookeds on there, but there's only a few names scribbled on, under the yellowing page-three girl who's been pinned on that board for over a decade.

'I might nick to the shops a moment actually, Lynsey, while I'm waiting.'

She keeps her eyes on the screen a few seconds before turning round.

'Whatever ye like, Mick, that's fine. I'll tell Malc ye've been by, will I?'

'Do, please, Lynsey. I'll be back in a wee while just.'

He leaves the office, giving a keek into the workshop as he turns toward the lane, where he can see Bertie, chatting with Steve and a young-looking guy that he can't see the face of.

Crapbag. He's a genuine crapbag and no other word for it.

He is in a bar near to work. He came in because it looked quiet through the window, and he was just wandering about, no sure where to take himself. Crapbag. These are his friends, christsake; well, if no exactly friends then his co-workers at least and that's something, sure that means something. Even now, it does. And no like they don't have their own problems to deal with. Steve, with the wee daughter's illness; Bertie, and his troublesome relations with the drink. Sure Bertie would be good for a patter; if there's one thing he's got still, it's his patter, even if he's lost the rest. Amazing to think now, how he used to be. The figure he was forty years back almost, during the work-in. A five-foot queerie with jug ears – no way anybody would ever have thought he could hold a crowd the way he did – but when he was stood up on his brazier with a hundred black squad around him, he'd have the whole yard in his spell. The high wheedling voice, beeling at the government, two hundred clatty ears hanging on his every word. The guy could go on for

69

hours. It was the likes of Bertie that kept them going: even when the redundancies were announced, they stayed put inside the yard, kept building, didn't let the liquidators or any other of these bastards past the gateman; and all through that winter and into the next spring Bertie and the other shop stewards would still be there to hand them their wages. The campaign fund keeping strong; the wives and girlfriends bringing them their food parcels. Cathy and her piles of ham rolls wrapped in newspaper, passing them to him over the barrier.

Hard to believe, looking at it now – at Bertie, old and trembling – that they'd won.

He gets up and goes to the bar for a final drink.

'Half and a half,' he tells the barman, watching as he reaches up to the gantry for his whisky. Christ but the drink makes him maunderly. These will definitely be his last. A maunderly old crapbag, is what he is, and he grins to himself, the guy coming over with his beer and his whisky. He's a great beardie young fella, with small sore-looking eyes like a pair of arseholes, and an oversized T-shirt that says VAGITARIAN – one of they ones you only ever seem to see extra-large guys wearing. He puts the drinks on the bar top and Mick pays and goes back to his seat in the empty room. A cruel bastard, ye can be, Mr Little. A cruel auld bastard and ye know it. Aye, I do, I do, but see that's the drink to blame again, if the truth be told.

An unexpected turn of events: he has found himself in an electrics megastore. How he's ended up here it's hard to say, and given that the stumbliness of the drink is taking effect and that he isn't actually needing a new iPod the now, it probably isn't the most sensible destination. It's woke up the security guard though.

Nay chance he's going back into work now. That is obvious enough. No with the length of time he's been out for, and the smell of alcohol on him. He walks around at random, half aware of the guy watching him. There's golf on the televisions all down this aisle he's in, dozens of them all showing the same event: one of these sponsor's tournaments with a few pros playing round with rich men and celebrities – retired footballers and elderly film actors, that type of nonsense. Alan would love it. He's probably watching it the now even. Christ he's probably playing.

There is laughter somewhere. It's hard to tell where it's coming from, how far away it is, but it is a man and a woman. He has grown to recognize the voices from hearing them talking together some-times if it's a warm day outside. They were arguing earlier the after-noon but now the sound is clearly of laughter, finding its way in under the door and through the cracks in the window frame.

He is cold. He has lain there with the covers pulled up all morning and there's nay chance he's tweaking the door open so he'll have to live with the smell just – the clinging stink of a fish supper he brought back a few days ago. A while later but he is too thirsty, and he does get up, leaving the shed to go for a drink of water from the kitchen. He is turning the tap when the phone starts ringing in the lobby. It startles him. He stays there, frozen, with the tap still run-ning and his arm beginning to shake. It rings a long time. He waits for it to finish and he turns the tap off, putting the mug on the counter, and leaves straight out the house by the front door.

Maybe he'll take a walk down the water. Keep moving; he needs to keep moving.

He isn't too sure the time, or even what time is safest to come these days and what's best left alone, it's that long since he's been down. So he comes slowly up the path, scanning up the way ahead. There is a young couple he comes past, with their two tiny weans. One of them is in a pram, and the other running about, scampering between the headstones and her da trying to coax her back. She's got the right idea but. Why no run about the place, instead of teetering around the graves? They're dead, christsake, they're no bloody sleeping.

There's new flowers again. The ones Mick left himself are there next to them, gone dry and brown by now. He picks them off the plot and gets them slung over the palings. Strange Craig's left them there, although – no, see even that is probably done on purpose, as a reminder, a marker of the da's last visit. That's exactly the kind of thing he would do, in fact.

It's started drizzling, so he walks over by the palings and stands under a bit of tree. See what makes it the worse is it's hard no to pity the boy. The same useless fucking pity that everybody's so keen to stick on him, he's doing it too, when he imagines him up there in Yoker alone and angry, naybody to talk to. Or maybe he does. Who knows? There had been a girl he was seeing, Tina, was she called, but there's no way of telling if they're together still. Maybe not, in fact. It had seemed like something of a loose kind of arrangement, from what Cathy had said. He should ask him. He gives a short laugh at the idea. He's only once before been up to see him, and that was a few years ago. Into the dingy flat boufing with dirty plates and filled-up ashtrays, but no his place to say anything, so he didn't; and neither did Cathy even because, as she says, it's his life to do as he wants and see if he wants to make mistakes then he'll make mistakes, and he'll learn from them, same as the rest of us.

The family are on their way, ahead of him as he leaves along the path. The wee girl holding her father's hand, and him leaning over and giving the wife a kiss on the side of the head. You don't think, when you're that age, about all this that might happen – that is going to happen, actually, a pure certainty it is going to happen. You're too busy with getting the food on the table and clothes on the weans' backs and feeding the wife's bingo habit to start thinking about what like it might be when one of you is gone. And too right. Jesus. Too right. What a thing to think about.

There is a man outside the house. Mick has turned the corner into the street and is coming up the pavement when he sees him, standing at the front door. Mick turns straight around. Keeps moving. Gets back down the end of the street to the bus stop and spies through the glass. He's still there, just stood, waiting. From here, he can't see properly who it is, but he's sure he doesn't recognize him. He fights to get the breathing under control. Maybe it isn't his house, and he's mistaken, it's actually next door. It isn't but. It's definitely his house. The man is peering in the window now, cupping his hands around his face. He chaps the door. Now what? Wait, just wait. The man turns and starts inspecting the grass at his feet, as if he's looking for something, and then he's up to the window again, spying in. For a second, a strange hopeful thought hits him that maybe it's a robber, but just then the man turns and goes out the gate and he can see his face. It's nobody he recognizes, a big guy in a shirt and tie, who is getting now into a dark red car parked on the street outside. It's a while before he leaves but. The car stays there another few minutes before it starts pulling out from the kerb and swings round, moving off in the direction away from the bus stop.

Mick waits a moment longer, watching carefully. As he gets up and starts toward the house, there is laughter, and he spins around to see two teenage boys knotting themselves looking at him from one corner of the bus stop. He walks away quickly, checking around him, and gets in the gate and then the house, hurrying through it and out into the garden, snibbing the latch of the shed as he comes inside.

II

The cold. It is setting in. Keep the whisky flowing, my man, keep it flowing. He unscrews the cap and takes another bolt – a bottle he'd minded was in the kitchen, unopened, laid out on top of the cupboards. A present from Alan last Christmas. The usual gift from him, but no complaints, he's bloody grateful, serious. The bottle carefully chosen, you can tell: decent enough it's obvious he's spent some money, but never a single malt, never something that the average man, in the brother-in-law's opinion, should be drinking. But fine. Fuck it. Fine. Cheers then to the brother-in-law and to his charming wife, who haven't as it happens been down once to visit the grave since they left. Which tells you everything, really, everything. Still but you can't have it all ways, eh, and the better that he doesn't have to see them; plus as well of course, how does he know for sure that they haven't been? Maybe they have, see, maybe they have. No way. They haven't. There would be some display of flowers or something. They have not been. See if they come at all, they'll come when it suits them. When there's a film they want to see, or they need a new computer.

A stifty wind in under the door. He pulls the blankets close. Jesus, he's hungry. He drags the emptied tool box from under the table and feels about inside it for the end of a packet of biscuits, then gets eating a couple. It's nearly finished, the food store. A battle plan needed. Another problem for another day.

He has had a pure stroke of luck. He'd been one afternoon rummling about in the back of the shed for anything useful there might be, and he found the wee battery radio they used to put outside sometimes when they were sat or she was at the gardening. It's still working. A miracle. And it's good too, having it on, no bother that the reception is pretty fuzzy, it's better than nothing, especially these nights he's laid there just, with the brainbox going, no able to sleep.

He listens to the quiet voice of the nightwatchradioman. He's talking about this TV programme that he watched the day about assisted suicides and people going away for them, the legalities and all that. Mick's no hearing it all, but it's relaxing, the sound of the guy's voice. There is a call-in after, but they don't stick to the topic. People can ring in saying whatever's on their minds. What do ye think will be the score Saturday? Barry in Pollokshields predicts a thumping away victory for the Gers, and a hat-trick for the new boy. Here's hoping, Barry, here's hoping.

The food store is gone. It's fine but, it's okay; no like it has come out the blue. He's been intending the last few days to go the messages for one or two items. Bread. Biscuits. Cheap things that don't need going in the fridge and he can keep out here. Another bottle of whisky would be much appreciated too, but he's got to be careful watching the pennies, got to start thinking where's the money going to come from. He closes his eyes. Got to do this, got to mind to do that. It's too much to think about. Easier to shut the eyes just and go to sleep, no have to deal with anything just now.

I2

Des is standing on the pavement out front of the Empress when he spots the distant figure of Mick approaching down the street. He drops his cigarette to the ground, picks up the broom that is propped against the wall, and gets sweeping the lunchtime dog-ends into the road. No that there's a great many. There'd only been a few in: the small group of staff from the recruitment agency round the corner, a couple of shopping-centre workers, and Pat, who is the only person left in the bar now, quietly drinking his Guinness over the racing odds.

He finishes clearing the pavement, and waits to say a hello to Mick if he isn't stopping in for a drink. Halfway down the street though, Mick crosses over and goes into the closemouth of a tenement on the other side, a blue carrier bag in his hand, and disappears. Des goes inside. He pours a refill for Pat, a Grouse for himself, then goes into the back for a sit down.

Maybe it had been someone else. Looked like Mick but. He sits back and lights a fag, keeping an eye through the bar to the lobby entrance. The family must have all gone by now: it's well over a month since Craig was coming by those nights, so he's obviously back up in Yoker. They might be on with a claim by now, from what Craig had been saying then. Awful fucking sad, what had happened. She was a great woman, Cathy, a cracker. Always had been. Back in the day, he used to have something of a crush on her. When he was a young guy first working the bar for his father, he'd look forward to her coming in with the other women during the work-in. There will be no bevvying, the shop stewards had told their men, so they were doing it for them, they'd joked. Just awful bloody sad. It could've been any of those women – still could be. The whole area is a timebomb. It could well be him next, or Pat, or any of the men that he'd stood and listened to from behind the bar, right from when there first started to be the rumblings, talking about it like it was something far off and no to do with them, even though they were sat there with the dust caked in their ears and their arseholes. A customer is coming into the lobby entrance. Des gets up, reluctantly wedges his fag in the ashtray, and goes through to the bar.

Mick comes back into the shed with a wee feeling of triumph and puts the items into the food store: bread and biscuits, a packet of cheese, tinned apricots and luncheon meat; even a paper for something to read and while away the hours. See all that stupit carry-on and then in the end it was fine. He's probably only been gone twenty minutes. He gave the Co a swerve, so all he did was get to the cash machine on the high street, draw out a note and ignore the fact the account is gone overdrawn, then dot in the minimarket on his way back for all these bits and pieces. Easy-oasy.

Now that it's done he steps out of the shed again and sets his sights on the house. He may as well get everything done in one go, collect more plates, a knife and a fork, and fill up the watering can with fresh water. Then he'll be set.

He stands outside the shed and looks down the line of back gardens, all empty; wet leaves and rubbish strewn about. Five minutes and he'll be done. Put the blinkers on, get in and get out. He starts toward the house. Grey pebble-dash; green back door. Strange but he doesn't recognize it, it's that unfamiliar somehow. If he'd been in the shed and he'd tried thinking what colour is the back door, what colour is the front door even, he wouldn't have been able to say, serious, he wouldn't. All they details: doors, carpets, furniture, they all merge into a general feeling you have, a habit, of being in the house. A place you return to at the end of the day after your toils, and relax. The familiar routines – putting your keys on the counter, sticking the kettle on, getting sat in your chair – it's natural just, you don't even think about it. All of it so far past the now. Gone. None of it fits.

The bulb is out in the kitchen. He goes to the cupboard for plates, working by the dim light coming in through the rain-smeared window. Grey shadows on the counter from the kettle and the toaster. He gets a cup, a knife, fork, then he rinses out the watering can; gets filling it with clean water. What would be a good idea as well is pulling the covers off Robbie's bed: the nights are too cold getting, even with the extra blankets he's brought out. He goes out of the kitchen and it's the speed of things, the combination of them all happening together, that undoes him. The light no turning on. The tide of envelopes by the door. A noise upstairs – a bump. It all happens in a second, before he can get registering any of it, and his heart banjos right up his fucking throat and he has to shove against the banister, pressing his back to it and craning to look up the stair. His breathing is heavy and snatched, he can't control it. It is gone silent up there. But then there's another bump somewhere above his head; he makes a dart for the living room door beside him. Quiet as he can, he crouches down behind the settee and gets lying in the narrow gap between it and the wall.

His leg is murdering underneath him, but he doesn't budge. Still nothing from up the stair. The blood in his ears is making it hard to listen, but he strains to hear, ready for any sound in the ceiling above him. Stupit. He is trapped, and whoever it is that's up there is just waiting, because they know it, or they've went, or they weren't even bloody there in the first place, Christ knows. So he stays put, the leg aching and his knees pressed into the back of the settee. From where he's lying, he can see part of the video player under the television, but the display clock is blank so he can't tell how long he's been there, maybe only a few minutes, or maybe hours, who knows?

Quietly, stiffly, he gets himself out from the settee. His ears are pure bursting, he's listening that hard as he edges out from the room and into the corridor, quickening his pace, coming into the kitchen and grabbing the things before getting out the back door. He clicks it softly shut behind him. A quick look at the upstairs window before he reaches the shed, but there's nothing.

He is sat in the straight-backed hospital chair with the plastic peeling off it and the foam poking out, while she stares out of the window. The white curtain is pulled shut in a horseshoe around them, and there's the peaceful hum of a dozen sleeping, snoring, dying women in the room outside. Through in the corridor, the faint hurrying patter of nurses' feet. And beyond the window, where she's staring, a gardener, whistling himself a tune as his pink head tots in and out of sight behind a hedge. After a while he comes round the near side of it, and he's got his shirt-sleeves rolled up, it's that sunny a day. The windows are open, and it's awful welcome, the freshness of the air outside coming in with his wee tune, pouring into the stale room. All of a sudden there is a fart somewhere outside the curtain – a loud, long, trumpety job – which causes him to chuckle and look at her, but she hasn't noticed it, she's still fixed on the gardener. She has been asleep all morning and she's lying restfully the now as he sits quietly watching her.

A nurse pops her head through the curtain at one point, gives him a smile and disappears again. She didn't signal she was coming in, it occurs to him when she's gone. But then what would be the point? She is the one that's changing her clothes, helping her go to the toilet. There's no need being discreet any more; it's past that. Maybe if he'd been sat there himself in the bare scuddy, his balls sticking to the seat, then maybe she'd start giving the signal. He grins. Aye, probably.

There is the gentle hushed sound of a relative talking. Outside, the gardener is lopping the heads off a line of finished flowers at the bottom of the hedge. Still the bright, tireless whistle. He looks at her. Is she listening? Can she hear it? He realizes then that he doesn't know if she can or not – if she's listening, if she can see him, or if she's just staring out at nothing. And that is when he understands. It's the precise moment, in fact. Maybe she can hear it, maybe she can't, but either way it doesn't make any difference because it's only time now, only time that is in the way. He stands up from the chair to move toward her, and her eyes shift to take him in. He smiles, and brushes the headscarf back to give her a wee kiss on the forehead; then he leaves out of the cubicle to go and get a coffee from the machine down the corridor.

13

The biscuits are gone stale. There is the dull snap of wet fibreboard about them now, and the cheese has broke out in green spots and a white frilly moss. He opens the door a nook, pushing against the sludge of wet leaves gathered against it, and slings out what's left for the birds. No use it going to waste.

The shed isn't best equipped for this rainy period that's come on. It gets in under the walls and the door, and drips down off the window. The blankets are pretty damp getting by now. Probably he'll come down with some horrendous illness and go the way of the cheese. The sparrows the first to find him, to notice he's copped his whack when they start pecking inside on the lookout for food.

Enough of that. Talk about maunderly. Jesus.

He is running out of shit pits. There's nay chance he's going back in the house, with its strange atmosphere and its lack of lights and its mysterious bumping noises up the stairs, so that just leaves the bucket at the back of the shed. He did consider using it before, when he stopped using the house toilet, until he came to his senses and realized that would be mental. Instead, he'd took a corner of the garden, the border on one side where Cathy used to plant her flowers, and used a trowel to dig a line of small pits, each with the mound of soil next to it to cover over after he's took a crap. But now the line is almost filled. And as well, he needs to get some toilet roll. All he's got left to use is torn out half-pages of the *Southside News*. A delicate operation, serious, though it doesn't make much difference how gently he does it – the backside is getting sorer, and blacker, pasted each day with new articles about tenement regenerations and Roma beatings.

There is a noise coming from outside. A faint, distant, rolling sound. He thinks at first it might be the wind, which is piping cold pea-shooters at his feet from under the door, but he understands after a while that it's Ibrox. There is a match on. He tunes in the radio, but the commentary isn't the clearest so he gives that up and listens outside just, waiting for the wind to blow him a favour. It does, and a few times he hears a muffled roar going up. Maybe the new boy is on form. Taken the league by storm this past couple of weeks and making mincemeat of opposition defences. Whatever the score is, it seems like they're winning, and the result is confirmed for him later, because there's car horns pamping in the night, together with what sounds like a brawl away on the high street.

14

Here they come, the wee chaps. He listens, enjoying the sound of it, as they begin skittering on the concrete outside the shed door. Something aye comforting about the noise of them pecking the ground, tapping, the odd time, on the side of the shed.

Until recently there'd just been the one – probably the same patient guy that's been coming all the while – but he's obvious gone and let dab to all his mates that they can come and eat here, and now there's a whole mob of them. Good for him, no keeping it all to himself. Obviously no an English bird. A genuine Southsider, that sparrow. It's mostly just bread he's buying now, each few days when he works himself up to leaving the shed, and he keeps a couple of slices from each loaf aside to put out for them. Sometimes, when he hears them arrive and gets open the door latch, he lays a short trail of crumbs from the outside, into the shed, to see if he can get any of them to come in. There's one time, he managed it. This tiny head, poking in the door and then following the line, unaware, or otherwise unbothered by the great hulking creature that was keeping still and watching him from the darkness under the table. Sometimes as well he tries to sneak a look outside at them, but each time he does they all fly off, and he has to wait a few minutes until the noise starts again: that small fluttery sound of them out there, getting beasted into their breakfast.

15

A dark red car is turning off the high street. It comes past the park and the cemetery, slowing a moment for a pair of old women to cross the road, then continues on until it pulls into a residential street, and a few seconds later parks up against the kerb. A short bald man gets out, followed by a larger, younger man in a pullover. They come through the gate to Mick's house and stop by the front door. The older man knocks firmly, while the other peers into the living room window. There is no response from inside the house so the older man hunkers down and looks through the letterbox. In a moment he stands up and pushes an envelope through the flap. Then the two men, without speaking, go back through the gate, get into the car and leave.

On the other side of the house, in the shed, Mick is sitting up close to the radio. It is almost out again, the sound distorting quietly like voices inside a hull. He needs batteries – all the ones that were in the house are used up; more bread as well; cash. For now he clicks the radio off and gets the few remaining pages of the paper over for another read, nothing else to occupy his mind now that the morning is by and the sparrows have finished their breakfast and left.

**FIRST TENANTS MOVE IN TO NEW
HOUSING ASSOCIATION
DEVELOPMENT**

**SLOVAK ROMA COMMUNITY
GIVES A HAND TO SOUTHSIDE
CLEAN-UP**

**LOCAL LOLLIPOP MAN HAS REAL
STAYING POWER**

He gives a read of that one:

> Britain's top football juggler broke the record for keepy-uppies on Tuesday, when he kept a ball aloft for six hours at Debenhams in the St Enoch's city-centre shopping mall.
>
> Sadly, his effort was declared unofficial because there was no representative from the *Guinness Book of World Records* present at the event, although Graeme, 45, has still raised thousands for charity.
>
> Afterwards he said: 'I could have kept going but I had to stop because the store was closing.'

Mick gives a wee smile. Good on ye, pal. The thought of him there in the Debenhams, a crowd of skiving weans and confused old hens gathering round. 42,500 keepy-uppies. Fucksake. That's just mental. Interesting but, these stories that you hear. This other one he minds – about a restaurant owner with a rat problem: they're eating into his food stores and frightening the customers. See but these rats are too canny for the traps, and when they do eat the poison it isn't strong enough to kill them, so the guy decides he's going to leave his cat there the night in the hope the rats will start crapping it and scarper. So he locks the cat in the restaurant, and when he comes in the next morning he finds it out the back court, on top of the beer crates, devoured, only the poor creature's carcass left, and even then some of the bones are away.

Where'd he heard that story? Robbie, was it? Aye, it was – he'd been telling them while they were watching the TV, Lynn shifting about on the settee with a look on her like she'd just sat on a dod of crap, and Jenna elbowing at Robbie telling him it's no an appropriate story to be saying; but him carrying on anyway, nay doubt enjoying putting the mix in.

Probably he's been calling, Robbie. Likely he will have gave Craig a call too, asking him what's the story with the da.

He doesn't want to think about any of it though. It's more than he's up to the now; what he needs to concentrate on is this immediate situation in front of him. First things first, he needs cash, and that means bulling up to go into the bank to see about an overdraft.

He walks quickly, taking the back ways where he can until he has to come out onto the high street. He goes a short cut before the Empress, through a tenement close. There's nobody about. The door to a garbage cage is flapped open and the wheelie bins strewn all at angles inside it from the binmen coming collecting the morning. He comes down a side street and stops at the entrance to the high street, eyeing left and right. It's hoaching. It must be lunchtime: schoolweans outside the chip shop; traffic hurtling – and then, just his bloody luck, he keeks the woman from next door, pushing a pram on the far pavement. He retreats back into the side street, head down, observing the feet. Maybe she wouldn't recognize him even. There is some sort of oil smear down the one trouser leg, he notices, starting above the knee and staining all the way down to his shoes. Perfect. See there's him trying to keep the head down and remain unnoticed, but just look at the state of him – he's bloody bogging – he may as well be wheeling her along after him with a flashing light on top the coffin.

He looks up and watches the neighbour away down the pavement; the messages done, off back now to get on with the business of looking after the snapper, the husband no about, seemingly. And where is the husband? How come you never see him about? Easy to think the worst sometimes but maybe it's just that he's off on the rigs or something, you never know. Cathy would have known, sure enough, but otherwise you never know. There is a lull in the traffic and pedestrians, and he steps out onto the pavement.

When he gets there, the bank is queued out. He decides that he's best waiting until after lunch, and turns the other way down the street.

Which is how he finds himself in the library. It isn't what he intended, but he'd no been intending anything, and it looked quiet inside, so in he went.

She's very helpful, the girl at the desk. He can't have made himself awful clear when he came in, stood there staring just, not knowing if he needed a ticket or anything to go in.

'Can I help ye there?'

'No. Aye, well, see I'm just hoping to have a look round at the books.'

'Ye been here before?'

'No.'

'Come on well and I'll get ye up and running.'

She lifts the desk counter and he follows her as she gets showing him all the different sections while he shuffles behind picking books out at random, trying to seem like he's interested in them and he isn't just in there because he's too feart of everybloodywhere else. And it's good too, somebody being kindly that he doesn't know, who doesn't know him, who isn't sticking the whole pity routine on him. By the time she leaves him at it, he has a whole pile of books that he hasn't a clue what they are. He sits down and opens one of them, all the time looking about to see if anybody is watching him. No danger of that but. It's pretty empty in here. There is a guy that looks like he's a scaffer asleep with a newspaper spread out under his forehead, and three old hens at a table in the corner, each with a copy of the same book. Quite an animated conversation they're having.

'. . . he's clever, I think, he just doesnae get the credit, ye know. All these people that used to come on the show, and he could talk with any of them.'

'Aye, and he's awfy handsome too, say what ye want, but he is. Especially when ye look at the wife there next to him, she's that weary-looking.'

'Aw, come on, of course she's weary-looking – the man's a balloon!'

The three of them start chuckling.

'He is, Helen, he's a bloody balloon.'

The scaffer is woken up. He's got a pen and he's started ringing the classifieds, working down the column, putting a circle around every one. Fair play to him. I admire your confidence, my man. See really that's what he should be doing himself, having a look what jobs are going. If he can't deal with going into Muir's, then he'll have to think of something else, because he can't exactly live off nothing. What money they had, they used up while she was ill, and an overdraft is only going to last so long. A new job. Maybe move somewhere else. A different town. He turns the idea over for a moment. A wee flat somewhere he doesn't know anybody, with only a few simple things he needs in it – TV, kettle, heater – new, replaceable things.

The thought of Muir's, and seeing Lynsey again after he'd done the run-out last time. What they must be saying about him. His chest starts to tighten and he has to concentrate on his breathing, try to control the panic. Across the way, the guy is still going through the columns, ringing the lot, and he wonders if maybe he's some kind of headbanger. But then maybe he's just in here for the same reason he's in here himself. This is his place of refuge, where people leave him in peace and he doesn't have to worry about the outside and all the rub-ye-ups. That's him the now too. Another headbanger in the library. He stands up abruptly to leave, making sure to thank the lassie on the desk and picking up a copy of the *Southside News* as he goes out.

It is quiet in the bank, only a few people queuing up and two clerks on. Nobody he recognizes. He has to collect himself, get it done with, get it over, go back to the shed. The recorded voice calls him to a window. There is a young guy behind the glass. His neck is pinched and red, bulging out from his collar.

'I'm wanting to see about an overdraft.'

'Okay. Pass me your bankcard please.'

He takes it out of his pocket and drops it in the drawer. Across from him there is a dithering old guy stood at the next window – 'Ma what?' – and then the voice through the glass: 'Your statement, sir, I need to see the statement.'

'The account is in debit.' The clerk is looking at him.

'I know. That's how I'm wanting to see about an overdraft.'

He goes back to his screen, tapping away at the keyboard.

'See, I'm afraid there isn't the option of an overdraft on this type of account.'

'Okay, right.'

That's that well. He looks round and the old guy is still rummling shakily in his mac pocket for his statement, pulling out streams of tissue, coins, bus tickets. When he turns back to the window, the clerk is tapping at his keyboard still.

'It might be best, in your circumstances, looking into if you can get a new type of account. I could give you some information.'

So there it is, then, even the bank knows – it's there on his screen.

'I'll leave it the now, thanks.'

Hunger. No surprise there. He lays in the dark looking up out the window at the moon, big and bright the night. The food store is empty. Him and the sparrows finished the last of it for breakfast so now he's pure starving, and you'd think he would be feeling some kind of urgency about the situation but he's not – no a great deal anyway – it's in fact more a kind of relief now that he's no money left. Strange. Figure that one out. No money, no food, and no chance he's going cap in hand to anybody. The idea of that knots him up – obviously it isn't an option – but he allows himself for a moment to imagine it, some kind of odd pleasure from kicking his own head in. Going to Pete for a lend of some money. Anything we can do to help, Mick. Anything we can do. Except fucking for that, Jesus Christ, are ye cracked?

But of course the brother-in-law, that's a different story: he'd be pure delighted, guaranteed. A great song and dance over it, the cere-monious fetching of the chequebook, the smug showy putting on of the wee reading glasses. How much would you like, Mick? Really, it's not a problem. How much? And going on the broo is out the question too. The thought of that is almost as bad as the thought of going to those other two. Queuing up with the wine-moppers, fill-ing out forms and forms and killing her over and over with each one. The same as it would be with the compensation. Deceased. Deceased. Deceased.

He'll be fine. He'll find a way. No like it's the first time he's found himself without any money, that's what he's got to mind, and this time as well it's just him, there isn't a whole family to support. Nothing could be as bad as the last time, when the job Alan had got him after Australia eventually fell to pieces. All they weeks and months of will theys, won't theys, and then the first wave of redun-dancies starting. Dozens of meetings with the shop stewards and the union men, and all that talk of refusing to give them an inch, don't forget the spirit of '72 and all that, but in the end it came to nothing. That's exactly what they got. Nothing. Alan and the Bowler Hats making their arrangements for theyselves, and all the rest of them left out to dry. See that was a worrying time. The severance cheque didn't solve anything, and the wife's job obvious wasn't going to keep the four of them for long. The arguments they had. So ye won't even consider it, well? It's the damned pride, is what it is, Mr Little. Ye know Don Paton is gone on the broo, so Sheila tells me, and no drama. I'm no saying it's easy, I'm no daft, see I'm only saying this frequenting of the Empress every afternoon and sitting about the house like a pound of mince isnae helping anybody.

She was right, obviously. And her taking on more hours at the store, it was hardly fair, plus on top of that having to come home knackered after work to him there on the settee, grumbling and drunk. Again. After she'd went through all this with him fifteen years before. Her working and him on the bevvy. Desmond the only person who was doing any the better out of it, his bar mobbed with black squad the whole time, drinking and shouting and scheming their plans of attack, convincing themselves that things could be got back how they were. That they knew what they stood for. I am a shipbuilder. That right, eh? So what are ye now that the shipyard has copped its whack and the job is away? I am a shipbuilder. Once a shipbuilder, always a shipbuilder, and all that tollie they'd told they-selves. No just the jobs that went, but the life. Ordinary life, it was gone; it had to be admitted. Himself a culprit. One of the worst. He wouldn't let go. Couldn't cope with the idea that things had changed.

He turns over stiffly and pulls the blankets up to his chin. The nights are too cold now to sleep all the way through. A rain is start-ing, pattering above his head. He needs to figure something out. He will but. He's managed before, and he'll manage again. Before he eventually got in with the private-hire driving he'd had to leave town to do it, disembark to Newcastle, the short-term contract at Swan Hunter. You battle on just. That's what he'd done then, even if he did spend most of that time lonely and drunk, and it had been against her wishes in the first place. She'd not wanted to be left on her own, looking after the weans, but he'd done it anyway, the same as he always did, the same as when they went to Australia – had that been a joint decision? Had it hell. He'd told her that was what they were doing and so they did it. The moon there out the window. A full one. The great yellowy cunt, bright as a bare arse. Always his idea. Pack your things, hen, leave your job, your friends, your home – we're off! That's how it had been. His idea.

16

'Ye have the item with you?'

'Aye, it's just here.'

'Can ye put it in the tray for me please?'

He takes off his watch and places it in. She inspects it a moment, turning it about in her fingers. She's pure laggered in jewellery: her fingers and thumbs, a gold necklace, and these wee pearly bullets in her ears. Must be she gets a discount.

'Give me a moment please.'

She swivels out from her chair and goes through a back door, and he stands waiting in the empty shop. It isn't like he expected. What was he expecting? Christ knows. Not this, anyway. There's nothing antiquey about the place, that's for sure, all bright lights and a blaze of yellow in the display windows. Sour red carpeting and security notices on the walls. It's like a bank. Actually, no, it's even worse than a bank. He goes over to the window to look at the pieces. Hundreds of rings and bracelets, each of them their own sorry story. In fact, see why don't ye just go and slit the wrists in the corner here – ye may as well if ye're in the mood, ye maunderly auld bastard, christsake. There is a dull chap on the security window as the woman returns.

'Twenty pound.'

'Serious?'

'It's quite worn.'

'No, mean, it's more than I thought.'

She smiles. 'Want it back, well?'

'No, no, it's okay, thanks.'

She is still smiling as she takes out the money and puts it in the tray.

A grey, dreich day outside, the tops of the multis merging into the clouds and the sound of car tyres hissing up water as they come past. Twenty quid. He should probably feel pleased but he's too bloody starving, on the approach now to a minimarket for a sandwich.

The watch was a fiftieth birthday present from the other drivers at Muir's. It must have been pretty expensive if he was getting twenty for it now. That birthday – him, Cathy and the boys, they'd went to a restaurant in the centre. He tries to picture her, but he can't. It was just before Robbie left for Australia because Craig was digging him up the whole time – gonnae send Kylie my love and all this – he wouldn't leave it alone. They'd sat at a table in the corner and she'd been next to him, the place full and noisy, the waitresses with these old-fashioned aprons on and Robbie awful cheeky getting with them, to Craig's annoyance. He can't see her though. He knows she's there sat right next to him but she's the only part of it that's a blank.

He gets his sandwich, and he walks over to the cemetery to go sit down on one of the benches and eat it.

Still a blank. The familiar tightening of his body coming on and he has to relax. He has to relax. Normally he can do that in here, that's aye how he comes, but he's no helping things rubbing himself up like this; he should just calm it down, eat his sandwich. Craig. Craig is here. He's going up the footpath. The first instinct is to duck the head. He's walked right past him, and now he's away up the path toward the grave. Did he see him? Impossible to know, he might've, he might, how could he not've – he's come right beside him. The heart going mental. His body rooted to the spot, but nothing he can do: he can't get up because that will obvious draw attention to himself so all he can do is stay put and hope he doesn't turn round. He gives a keek up. The back of Craig's jacket, a way up the footpath now. He watches as the boy passes through a line of trees to the next lawn and stops when he reaches the grave. He's got his work clothes on, by the look of it, although it's hard to tell from this distance. He's just standing there, looking down. Me and you, Maw, it's me and you against all the rest of them. He stands there a minute or two before he starts to bend and crouch down, and as he does so he turns his head. He is looking straight toward him. It's a bare instant just, a single second, then he turns back to the grave.

He flicks the light switch out of habit but of course it doesn't come on, but so what, he doesn't need to see any of it, the less he can see in fact, the better. As it is, he can still make things out in the half-dark. The mound of post at his feet; the bare, ripped ribbon dangling off the wall. This needs to be done quickly, or if not he's going to collapse in a heap no able to get up and that'll be that, never to be seen again. Except by the man up the stair, of course, that bastard – he needs to be calm, concentrate – no think about a man up the stair. He keeps it all blanked out as he goes through the kitchen, fetching a carrier, and then gets up the steps to the bedroom. He moves quickly inside. Ignores the dark heap on the bed. He pulls open her drawer and grabs a handful of jewellery, dropping it into the bag. His breath is snatching now, coming in jolts, but he's managing it, he's coping, taking another couple of handfuls to empty the drawer, and the truth is it feels good – there – so fucking what? What difference does it make anyway? She's dead. She's not going to wear it.

He'd be pure raging if he knew. But he doesn't, and he can get to fuck if he thinks he's got any more right to her than anybody else. He goes out of the room and back downstairs, where he gets his jacket and the small battered holdall from the lobby, and starts putting things into it: the carrier of jewellery, then out to the shed for his change of clothes and the newspaper. Then he's away. Gone. Goodfuckingbye.

'Ye back, then?'

'I've brought some more things.'

'Go on, well, let's see.'

He empties the carrier into the tray. She gives him a look but he ignores it, and he stares away toward the window while she inspects through it.

'Is it for loan or sale, this?'

'Sale.'

'Okay, well we buy gold and silver by the gram, so I'll need a wee while to price this lot up, that alright?'

'That's fine. I'll wait.'

She gives him £250 for all of it. It's worth a lot more, he knows, but no like he has much of a choice. There's a ring in there that used to be her grandmaw's, which must be worth a couple of hundred on its own, plus a few other things that were handed down to her when she was a wean in a big house in the Highlands and she hadn't yet disgraced and ruined herself with the dirty plater husband.

It's pishing it down when he gets outside. He could get on the subway, all this cash he's got on his tail now, but he needs to be careful saving it so he waits for a bus instead, standing a long time with the wind blowing in and water dripping off his nose. He gets the next one into the centre and gets off at the coach station. There is only a short queue at the ticket desk.

'When's the next coach to London?' he asks the guy.

17

There is a bronze statue by where the man waits. A life-size young couple greet each other, a bag on the floor beside them, and he is lifting her up, their lips about to meet, one hand sliding down over her bottom. The man smiles, looking at it. A couple of girls come past and notice the statue; they start giggling. His own bag is not much bigger than the bronze man's. In it, his few clothes, his work boots, a plastic wallet with his valuables and a little food for the journey. Already there is a large group waiting by the glass doors for the London coach, but he sits further off, on a plastic orange seat by the statue.

He goes inside his coat for his phone and makes a call.

'Yes?'

'Yes, my name is Juraj. I am arriving in London tonight.'

'Got an address?'

'Yes.'

'Passport?'

'Yes,' he lies.

'Right. You'll find details where to come in the morning. There will be a van waiting. Bring the passport, and the driver will need your expenses up front. He'll take you straight to the site.'

'Okay. Okay. The flat is not shared? My wife and son come here soon. The other man said it is not shared.'

'No, not shared. Polish?'

'No. I am from Slovakia.'

'Right, well. Plenty of Polish there. Slovak too probably. You come at six tomorrow. Details are in the flat.'

He puts the phone back in his coat and continues to wait for the coach. Things will not be easy once he arrives; he is not stupid. When the agency in Slovakia arranged for him to come to Glasgow, they told him the same thing. You will have your own room. It will be comfortable for your wife and child when they join you. And on the outside, the red brick building did look beautiful, if you ignored the – 'Govanhell' . . . 'Fuck off gypos' . . . 'Scum' – local poetry. He could not bring them to a place like this. Five cramped streets: no privacy, no heating, no landlord. White and Asian gangs. In London, at least, they will be hidden – Roma, Polish, Pakistani – nobody will care.

An old woman is standing in front of the statue. She looks at it for a moment, then moves away to where a line is forming in front of the glass doors. Back home, it is getting more dangerous: last month, his wife's brother was badly beaten and left in the tip next to where they live. There is no choice now but for them to come here; it is the right decision. The driver is opening the doors and climbing onto the coach. He stands, picks up his bag and goes to join the queue.

There are no empty pairs of seats left on the coach, so he sits down next to a man who is staring out of the window with his hands on top of his bag, clasping it to his lap. Past the man's head, he can still see the statue through the glass wall of the station, and he continues looking at it until the engine starts up and the coach rolls off. He grins. When my wife arrives here, he thinks, this is how I will touch her bottom.

A young guy with a shaved head is come and sat in next to him. It's okay but. He doesn't look like the type that's going to be chinning him all the way down for a conversation. Which is good, because it's a long-enough journey. More than nine hours. Arriving in London in the wee hours, when the pubs are shut and the cafes aren't yet open. He could've planned it better, serious. He could have planned it at all, in fact.

By the time they get leaving the city and the sudden leap of green at the end of the schemes, the gloaming is come on outside the window and he is falling asleep. When he wakes up the lights are turned off and it takes him a moment to mind that he's on a coach, people snoring around him, a dim strip of lighting along the aisle floor, fallen crisps and a crisp packet and legs stretched out. He looks out of the window into the rushing darkness. He doesn't feel jittery. He feels okay. He doesn't feel anything.

A while later and the neighbour is awake. Mick can hear him shuffling forward and unzipping a bag down by his feet. The sound of paper, or plastic, tearing. Then the smell of food, a sausage roll, which he brings up to his mouth and starts eating. Okay, well, a plan. The first thing when the coach gets in is to eat: probably he'll have to find a petrol station or a 24-hour minimarket and wait in the coach station until everywhere else starts opening up. Then onto the job hunt. For starters, this one he's seen in the *Southside News*.

The guy is looking across at him.

'You know where is King's Cross?' he asks, as if they've been pattering away all this time.

'I've no idea, pal, sorry. I've no been to London before.'

The man nods and carries on eating his sausage roll, then after a while he gets out his mobile phone and starts thumbing away. It's a pretty decent point – does it matter that he's never been there before? No, it doesn't. That's the best bloody thing about it. He needs to keep things simple. Keep away from any reminders. Go see about this job advertised in the paper and get on top of himself, fix things out. Englandshire. Nobody will guess that one. He's only been twice before: the six months in Newcastle was the last time, and way before that, when they weren't long married, a visit to Cathy's cousin and the husband in Northampton. Fucking terrible. There were a few of her relatives set up in England, and they'd spent a miserable week with these, himself going about the place trying no to spill and break things and none of her lot speaking with him unless it was to ask him stupit questions about the yards, that same way people use when they ask a wean how school is going. They didn't come to the funeral, that pair, as far as he can mind.

It is raining. He sits back and looks at the giant windscreen wipers going back and forth on the front window. Thinking about England. Newcastle. How he'd felt going down this very motorway, moving further away from home; the argument that him and Cathy had got into the night before he left, both of them shouting, Thatcher on the television in the background, bringing the poll tax to Scotland. See in truth he'd been lucky getting a job at all, because Swans had went the same way as everywhere else – privatized, shrunk – but he hadn't felt lucky; he'd felt fucking terrible. He'd rented a room in a house with quite a few Swans workers, young lads mainly, and a guy his own age from Southampton, he can't mind his name. They'd all go out together to the bars, come back and get the landlady raging. But the clearer memory is of the nights he'd spent alone in his room, drinking, wondering what in hell he was doing in this place. Sat there on his days off, the TV on, until it got too much and he'd go the long walk to the phone box a few streets away.

The neighbour is snoring. Mick turns toward the window, trying to shake the mood that has come over him. Remind himself it wasn't all bad. Because it wasn't. They were good men, for one thing. Mad for their football, anyway. There were always games down by the jetty after lunch; races up the bank by the young lads at the end of a shift; nicknames – Big Yin, they'd called him right from day one, because they knew Billy Connolly had worked on the yards. He never really felt part of it though. He couldn't, no with Cathy and the boys up in Glasgow. And it wasn't his yard; his river. He didn't belong there. Didn't get the same feeling from it: that sense of the river always being there, around him, inside him. The sheer thrill of a ship on its stocks, grown from just a few small pieces of metal, walking toward it each morning and seeing that it was bigger, looking like it was parked there at the end of the street, looming over the end tenement. He can mind exactly the feeling of it. The sound of the hooter. The gates opening and the mass of workers teeming through. Getting into the yard and seeing that the graffiti on the hull had been added to – jokes, patter, Proddy slogans – so that when the ship was near completion you'd look at her and the whole of her side would be a mess of chalk scrawlings. Comic pictures of the managers. Competitions of who could write the highest. Two-year-long conversations. And then, when she was built, it would all be painted over and there'd be no clue as to what was written underneath; except if you looked hard enough, the tiny scribbling along the waterline where the painters had wrote their nicknames.

The driver is pamping the horn to get everybody awake. Mick stands groggily, and presses into the line slowly moving down the aisle. As he steps off the coach, away into the terminal, it is the first chance he's had to see the other passengers. There's a fair number of East Europe types amongst them, it looks like. Something about the quiet way they get on with things, filing off to the exit and seeming to know exactly where it is they're headed – even the neighbour, striding off with his bag over his shoulder, King's Cross here I come.

There is a snack machine in the arrivals terminal and he gets himself a Mars bar, then sits down on one of the backless plastic seats, pulling his jacket tightly about him, and tries to get the brainbox working.

Somebody standing over him. A big fella with a meaty face.

'You okay there, mate?'

A sliver of belly poking out beneath the shirt.

'Do you know where you are?'

Mick chuckles. 'I've no got a clue, pal.' He notices then there's the half-eaten Mars in his lap.

'You can't stay here, I'm afraid.'

'It's fine, see I must've fallen asleep for a minute just. I'm looking for a cafe that's open, if ye know somewhere.'

'I do actually. There's one just round the corner, as it happens.'

He points Mick what direction it is and waits for him to get up and leave.

When he gets there it is open, like the man said. The pleasurable sound of chairs and plates and low conversation as he steps in and gets himself a table, reading the breakfasts off coloured sheets of card above the kitchen. A few coach-driver types drinking coffees. A street cleaner in a high-vis jacket, and he minds suddenly the incident with the parkie and the stolen flowers, but he shuts it out straight away as the guy comes over for his order. Bacon and eggs, and a tea. He's pretty friendly, the time of morning it is, humming himself a wee tune. Turkish, if the poster above the kitchen is anything to go by. Things have started well. A hot breakfast about to arrive, in a little wink-wink of a place that he's found, when instead he could easily be pounding about the streets right now for a petrol station.

When he's finished, he goes up the counter and asks the guy if he knows anywhere nearby he might get a room for what's left of the night.

'Hostel? B&B?'

'B&B, aye.'

He reaches for his order pad and pulls a pen from his trouser pocket, but then hesitates, deciding against it. He points an arm to his left.

'You see this street? You go down, you go left under the bridge, and there – there are many places. Ten minutes.'

Mick thanks him and picks up his bag to leave. No bad, eh, this London. No bad.

He can see the bridge up the way. It is a railway bridge, he can make out as he gets closer, walking alongside the high sooty walls that follow the road beneath. There is a narrow street just before the bridge and he turns onto it, past a builders' merchants and an MOT garage under the arches. A few minutes down and he spots a cracked white plastic sign: BED AND BREAKFAST: SINGLE £25, DOUBLE £40, FAMILIES £60. Fine. It will do. He just needs a bed for the night, it's no like he's choosy. He goes up the steps and there's no obvious buzzer so he tries the door, and it's open. He treads into a dimly lit corridor with a worn red carpet and the ribs of the floor-boards showing underneath. Yellow, chappit wallpaper. At the end there is a sign – RECEPTION – and an arrow pointing up the staircase.

He goes up to the first stairhead, where there is a door with a crumpled plastic file pinned on it. A piece of paper inside. *Back in 10 minutes*. It doesn't look likely. Probably it's too late the now to get somewhere, but just then a man appears on the stairs behind him, another Turk, by the looks of him.

'Have you lost your key?'

'No, I just, mean, I was hoping to get a room.'

The man leads him up the next flight of steps, fishing a bunch of keys from his pocket, and unsnibs a door.

'Single room?'

He nods.

'Single room is £25.' He stands there scrunching the keys down by his side. Ye reckon he wants the money up front, well? Mick gets out his wallet.

'Whereabouts is breakfast served?'

'No breakfast.'

'Eh? No breakfast? It says "Bed and Breakfast" on the sign outside.'

'No breakfast.' He takes his money and leaves.

No breakfast, then. Mick stands at the door and takes in his room. Poky, a stale clinging smell, the same peeling wallpaper as the corridors, and what looks like a giant shite-mark on the carpet. It's better than a shed though, so nay point complaining. There's no curtains, instead a grey veil pinned over the window with an orange glow coming in one side of it. He climbs onto the bed, which seems clean, and is that tightly tucked it looks vacuum-packed. He lies on top of the covers. He should be doing a stock-take of the situation, he knows, but his head is aching and it's hard to think clearly, so he lies there just, the eyes closed, vaguely aware of a streetlight buzzing outside, and at one point the rumble of a train going over the bridge.

Later the night he has to pee, the need for it building and building until it's too uncomfortable, and he gets up. He waits at the door a while, listening to make sure there's nobody about, then he comes out, and up the next flight of steps to a door marked BATHROOM. No that he wouldn't have telt it by the smell: sharp, sour, mixed in with bleach, the bottle of which is left out, sat on a ledge under the sink. When he's done he comes back in his room and snibs the lock.

Morning. He lies there a long time. His stomach is uneasy, and the whole of his body is aching like he's just come off a back shift. The streetlamp is turned off and daylight sifts dirtily through the window veil, exposing the room. That scunnery brown streak on the carpet, he can see now that it's a scorch mark. Christ. Ye dread to think.

A noise outside the door makes him jump. Somebody pounding down the staircase. Quietening down the next flight, quieter, then silence. His heart is racing at the suddenness of it. Just a noise. It was just a noise. Somebody running down the stair, it's nothing out the ordinary. But he is panicking and it's a struggle to get control of it as he presses the side of his head into the pillow, hearing the thump of blood in his ear. That's just the problem but – it *is* out the ordinary. No like he hasn't heard people running down stairs before, but no *here*, no in this place he hasn't.

Just a noise, just a noise.

But he's got nowhere to put it. A fucking noise, man – they've gone by now – but it's bouncing around inside him, unable to come to rest because everything else is jumbled up and bouncing around together, and he can't act or think normally because what *is* fucking normal? Answer that one. What is normal? There isn't a normal. He swings his legs over the bed and sits up. Everything racing and rushing. He is sucking for breath but it's no good, sitting up is making him feel boaky, so he lies back down again and gives up trying to stop it. Thoughts hurtling in, he can't keep them out. She is normal. That is what normal is. There, he's said it. But now everything is birling around and it's all to fuck because that's the thing he's been trying to steer clear of, thinking about the wife, and now he's let it in and there's no controlling it. *She* is ordinary life – she's as much a part of him as his legs or his stomach – and without her all the rest has lost the plot. The stomach fucking especially.

Cry, man. Just bloody cry. Nobody's watching. But he can't let himself – it's there, he can feel it in his throat like a furball, retching and stuck, but he's too feart to let himself. It'll just make him the worse. And then he definitely won't be able to stop, he'll be here the whole day bloody greeting.

There are voices in the room below. So what? He's staying in a Bed and Breakfast – well, a Bed – what do you expect, he'll have to deal with it just. He can't hear what they're saying but it sounds like there's a few of them, a family, because there's a baby shrieking or crying or making some kind of a racket. He gets up off the bed and pulls the table that's under the window over to wedge against the door. Then he gets back on the bed. No television, so no easy way to ward off the brain, except for sleep, closing the eyes and sleeping, he could sleep all day, he could sleep forever.

Later he goes down and gives another £25 to No Breakfast, who counts the money carefully and slides it in his pocket.

That night he sleeps fitfully, in and out, a lot of it just staring at the orange glow through the window.

The people down the stair are arguing. A woman shouting. It goes on for quite a long time and then there's a door shutting and it goes quiet. He needs to get some food. No easy thing going out into the day but. What he needs to do is just blank everything out, kid on that he isn't actually existing and do the zombie walk to wherever the shop is. Nobody knows him anyway. That's what he has to tell himself. Nobody knows him.

He finds a Costcutter after the bridge. There is a radio playing but he can't hear the words. He gets a damp pasty in a packet from the fridge, a couple of lager cans and a sandwich for later. He doesn't look up at the man as he pays. Another guy by the door as he goes out, sat behind a kiosk like some silent gremlin, selling phonecards.

The next few days he slips into a routine. Out to the shop in the morning, and forcing the food down when he gets back. Then sleeping and drinking and keeping the brain quiet until he has to go down and give No Breakfast his money. The wee patter between them: how's it going, pal? Oh, not too bad, thanks, business pretty steady at the moment thanks to you and as well the family downstairs. Good, good, I'm pleased. Clutching for a normal. It is some kind of an ordinary, however crap.

18

He opens the *Southside News* and gets to the page:

> Major hotel chain, UK airports: Glasgow, Birmingham, Manchester, London Heathrow. Staff wanted, all departments: Housekeepers, Food and Beverage Assistants, Breakfast Chefs, Kitchen Porters, Reservations Assistants. Live-in positions.

Work. Work is what he's came down here for, and work is what's going to get him back onto his feet. Spend too long without employment and what else are you going to do but occupy the whole time alone with yourself until the brain is turned to mince? That's another reason he'd never go on the broo. Work is busyness at least. So he needs to get off his bahookie and get some, get on the keel and give Robbie a call, because this keeping him in the dark cannot go on. And so what if he's never been a kitchen porter before? He can do it, he can lie if he has to, and it's perfect, really: something different from what he's done before, no reminders. Plus as well the money situation: he's running out.

He washes himself, or tries to anyway, with what little water he can bleed out of the shower head. Afterwards, a good examination of the face in the mirror. He could fine well do with a shave, but he doesn't have a razor. Still, it's long enough now that he has a decent beard on. A respectable beardie man, a Sean Connery type, that's the way he should look at it. Although being honest, respectable is probably up in the air when they get to looking at his clothes. He's got on the shirt and trousers that he had in his bag, but the problem is that both of them are crumpled as a toad's foreskin. See what he should do, he should probably give a phone down to room service and ask No Breakfast for a lend of the iron. He forces a smile at the idea of it. He feels okay. He feels fine. He is going to get on.

He packs his bag and leaves away into the street. What he needs is a good shovel of food, to keep him going the rest of the day, and where better to get it than at your man's down the way, the cheery Turk.

After eating, he gets negotiating the subway. Finding it is easy enough, although the actual thing itself is genuine a bit more complicated; a Rubik's Cube of colour-coded trickery compared to the one he's used to. He manages but. He is managing.

There is a young guy on the line of seats opposite him. He's got on a pair of tight blue trousers and pointed white shoes, his legs crossed over like a woman's. The pointy foot joggling in the air with the bumps of the track. He's reading a magazine with a cartoon drawing of two men on the front with comic stretched faces. He's about ages with Robbie and Craig. What would they make of him? Just then but the train comes to a halt and he has to concentrate to get hearing the driver, and he is able to stop the thought before it can develop. He needs to keep focused. The brain is a genuine minefield of all these thoughts that he's got to keep himself from thinking, for the moment at least, just for the moment, until he's got himself back on his feet. Then he can see where he's at.

The hotel is one of a fair number along a drag that he has to cross a great tangle of carriageways and multi-storey car parks to get to. It's huge – they're all huge – and ugly. A block of grey, stained concrete; the only colour is the massive lettering of the hotel's name above the doors. The woman that he speaks to on reception is friendly enough but.

'The operations manager is in a meeting until three,' she tells him after she's put in a call. 'Do you mind waiting?'

'No problem.'

The operations manager, it turns out, after he's waited a long while on a seat fixed to the table in an empty restaurant, surrounded by plastic plants, is a woman. She doesn't shake his hand. 'You're a kitchen porter,' she says, going behind the bar to make herself a coffee. 'You're not agency though?'

'No.'

'Do you have a CV?'

'No.' Great start. Bloody haddock. 'See, I was in the shipyards, and then my last job I was a cab driver. But when I was younger I used to work in kitchens. Hotels and that.' A pretty obvious lie. She is behind the bar still, looking at him as she stirs a sugar into her cup. It isn't the face of an impressed person.

'I saw the job advertised in a paper.'

She frowns. 'When?'

'A while back, actually.'

She comes out from the bar. 'Well, it's up to the chef anyway. Come this way.'

He follows her round a corner into a passageway where the carpet stops, and there is a pair of swing doors with small porthole windows. Blinding bright inside, mobbed with men in white jackets. She goes in and he waits outside, a tight feeling in his chest. Relax. Just relax. She is stood just inside the kitchen, and a tall man is coming over toward her. Behind him, at a gas range, one of the chefs is pouring a packet of something into a pan. The tall man keeks at him through the porthole.

'. . . is him,' he hears her say as the doors swing open. She walks off without looking round and the man is stood in front of him.

'You've not done KP before, then?' He is Irish. He's got baggy red and white checked trousers.

'No, mean, not for a while.'

'Scottish?'

'Aye, Glasgow.'

He folds his arms, narrowing the eyes and smiling.

'Here's the million-dollar question, then – Bhoy or Bluenose?'

Mick smiles. 'Bluenose.'

The chef gives himself a comic slap on the forehead. 'Fucking typical.' He grins. 'No, it's fine, it's fine, I don't give a shite. And you're the right colour anyway.'

He goes in the swing doors and Mick follows, keeping the head down and avoiding looking up at the other chefs. He reaches for a pen on top of a whiteboard by the door.

'What's your name?'

'Mick.'

He writes it down next to BREAKFAST: MICK WASH I.

'You've timed it well in fact – we had a guy left yesterday.'

105

They walk through the kitchen. He is staying calm. Heat, young men with shaved heads, the sound of a radio. They go past a heap of crates, and the kitchen throats into another room, smaller, dimmer than the main one. A very black man in dark green overalls is clattering a pile of frying pans into a sink.

'Eric, take this fella down to the staff rooms.' He turns to Mick. 'Take whatever one is free and get yourself settled in for today. Breakfast starts at six so get here just before and I'll sort you out some overalls,' he says, and leaves.

The black guy hasn't looked up from the sink, and Mick wonders a moment if he has understood. In a minute though he stretches off his rubber gloves and goes out through a fire door, the tap left running.

He follows behind him as they go down steps and through corridors, and it's becoming clear enough that your man here isn't going to speak, walking slowly ahead, the bare back of his neck shining under the fluorescent strips. At one point a stretch of tubing is out, and they walk on in near complete darkness until the next lit corridor, then down more steps, right into the bowels.

'Here,' the black man says, and goes back the way they came.

He is left in a long corridor with doors both sides. One of them is open, and he sees inside that it is a bathroom. He goes down the line of doors. Low music coming from one; snoring, another. Otherwise the place is silent. He stands there, wondering what is his next move. This is mental. Unreal. It's that far removed from reality in fact that it's hard to believe there's not some kind of chicanery going on, the auld brainbox playing tricks. But to these people it's just ordinary; he is ordinary even, that's the strangest thing. All of them – the manager, the chef, the kitchen porter – it's like they expected to see him here. He hasn't caused the barest ripple of an interruption. Go downstairs and go in your room and you're working at six the morrow, and everything just carries on as it was.

Somebody is coming out of a door down the way. A girl. She's in her pyjamas and barie feet. He stands there rooted as she comes toward him, and he's about to have to say something when she turns into the bathroom. She didn't seem to notice him even. What, are they on drugs, these people? He feels like he's totally lost his bearings, the quiet sounds of snoring and music and humming strip lights around him, a girl in her pyjamas, and he's losing track already if it's day or if it's night. The toilet is flushing. She comes out and starts walking back to her room.

'Excuse me,' he calls out. She doesn't hear him.

'Excuse me.'

She looks back blankly.

'Can ye tell me which of these is free, please?' He can see now that she's been asleep, the eyes half closed.

She shrugs her shoulders. 'I think maybe this one.' She points to a door by the bathroom, and pads off.

He pushes the door open slowly and the shapes inside become clearer as the light from the corridor filters through. The room is empty, the bed made. He finds the switch and the bulb takes a moment stammering on. It is like a compartment in a storage warehouse, threadbare and windowless; tiled drop ceiling. There is a sink and a chipped white Formica wardrobe, a waste bucket, a chair and a small table with an alarm clock, the hands pointing just the back of four. Unreality has hold of him now, carrying him numbly on as he arranges his few clothes in the wardrobe, takes off his shoes, puts them under the table and gets lying down on the bed. Careful. He needs to be careful. Too easy to get maunderly and think about things – the lack of daylight, for one, Christ – but actually what he should be thinking is good positive thoughts. He has found himself a job. He is on his feet. He has got himself what he was looking for. What was that, well? It was an anonymous room in a place with no reminders and no bastards to pity him or stick the boot on. The image of Craig in the cemetery comes suddenly to him, but he knows he has to shut it away, shut it right away. He looks about him. See if he gives the room a bit of a spruce up it might not be so bad. A mini television. Plants. Maybe he could knock a couple of plastic ones out the restaurant even – there ye go, now you're talking man, now you're bloody talking.

There is noise outside the door just before five: foreign voices, shouts, a woman laughing. Then it goes silent for half an hour, until all at once the noise returns and there's a few minutes of activity before it quiets down again. After that, there's just the occasional sound: doors shutting, a voice coming past, the flush of the toilet through the wall behind his head. Later the evening he leaves the room and finds his way eventually out of the hotel, making his way over to the terminal, where he gets a jacket tattie and a pint.

He doesn't sleep the best, so the early start isn't a problem. He is up at the kitchen for quarter to six, waiting in the potwash. Through in the cooking area he can hear the Irish chef instructing his shaven-headed team to get set up. After a few minutes he comes into the potwash holding a fryer smoking with bacon fat, and sees Mick standing by the machine.

'Shite, yes.'

He goes off a moment and returns with a pair of overalls. 'He'll show you, but it's easy enough. Wash 1 means you stand at this sink and scrub most of the crap off everything, then you stack it in these trays for him to put through the machine. And you clean the kitchen stuff.' He points at the bacon pan hissing in the sink.

There is nowhere to get changed so he puts the overalls on in there, on top of his clothes. And that is the first thing he learns: not to wear anything underneath. Within half an hour he is pure sweltering from his exertions and the heat of the machine. Wash 2 is fine but. He's got the right idea – just the bare black skin visible under his overalls whenever he bends down to stack something – he's genuine fine and breezy. No that he's said as much: he's hardly spoke a word since he came in. It isn't the same one as yesterday – he's taller, this guy, and he's fucking fast. It's hard work keeping up putting the plates and cups in the trays before he grabs and trammels them along the runners into the machine – the hoosh of steam as he pulls it down and sets it running. Thirty seconds and they come out dry, it seems, because he piles the lot straight up and takes it over to the racks. When he does speak, it's to tell Mick that he's doing it wrong – 'No. No' – and he'll stand in front of him and start stacking the trays himself. It's doable but. He is doing it. He is managing. First day on the job and he's on top of it.

It is a separate world but, the potwash. He'd've thought it would be different to this – all noise and shouting and Gordon Ramsay, waiters running about with their arses on fire – but it isn't. It's oddly quiet in there, cut off, just him and Wash 2 scrubbing and stacking, scrubbing and stacking. There is the clanging and jouncing of ovens and grills from in the kitchen, and each while a chef coming through, shouting, 'Hot pan,' but even through there, there's no noise, no patter. Strange. It's fine but. It suits him. Ye keep the head down, ye do your job. Scrub, stack; scrub, stack. The faces of waiters appearing at the hatch above the sink to dump the dirties on the ledge. You new, pal? What's your name? Good to meet you, how's it going? They don't speak. They don't see him even. Fine. That's fine. And there's something quite satisfying about the work as well – no exactly stimulating but it's mechanical, you get into a rhythm, repeating the actions, challenging yourself to get the pile down. The empty ledge. A wee pat-the-back moment of job satisfaction. See that, Wash 2? First shift but no messing, eh, no fucking messing about, look.

Of course but he's jumped the gun. There he is thinking he's such a big man for keeping his piles down, while there must be hardly anybody in the restaurant. It doesn't start coming properly until an hour in. Plate piles begin growing on the ledge, tall teetering columns of bowls and cups; the cutlery bucket swelling like a haemorrhoid; and the waiters finding their tongues at last, beefing that they've no space to put the dirties. He's not keeping up and he's soon enough sweating all over the place in a panic, desperate to get it down before the Paddy chef comes through and sees.

Wash 2 is fair agity getting with him by now, butting over to get the piles and stack them himself. And then, just when it's coming on the busiest, the baldies start barging in with all their pots and pans, fat-fryer baskets, chopping boards, long metal trays lined with burnt knickers of egg. His heart is racing. He gets rushing about, losing his scourer, piles increasing all around him. He trips on a heap of pans by his feet and near goes on his neck. Bracing his hands on the sink, he takes a couple of deep breaths, the black guy glaring over at him. Get beasted in just. Get the piles down before the chef sees, finish this shift – then he can put down a marker, then he'll know where he's at. He leans toward the machine, ignoring Wash 2, pulls over an empty tray and gets loading.

Toward the end of the service, as he's thinking it's started to quiet down, they begin coming with great long dishes and glass bowls in from the restaurant. He gets scraping them out, chucking leftover sausages and grapefruit segments into the bin, until one of the waiters starts going through him, saying he has to wait until they've cleared all the food themselves. It must get reused, he realizes. All of it, too, they clear the lot. Even the eggs, man, Christ.

By the time it's over he is pure wheezing, blowing for tugs. And that was breakfast – Christ knows what like the lunch service is, or dinner. Or if he has to work them all, either, that's another thing he's still in the dark about. Still but he got through it. His standards were up in the air quick enough, but he got through it – congealed crockery going straight in the tray and the scrub, stack of earlier turned into a dump, dump, dump. Fair unlikely that it was coming out the other side clean, but Wash 2 didn't seem too bothered, he just wanted to keep it moving through, the piles kept down, the waiters shut up. To keep their faces away from the hatch.

Wash 2 takes off his gloves and motions Mick to follow as he goes into the kitchen. The baldies are bent and kneeling, scrubbing inside the ovens. Wash 2 writes his hours on the board and hands him the pen when he's done.

'Dia, is it? Hello.' He holds out his hand. 'My name's Mick.'

It doesn't feel quite the right thing, a handshake, but the guy takes it, with a small nod of the head. 'Breakfast now,' he says.

Mick follows him into a bare, bright room with tables put together into two long rows. There is a queue of twenty or so staff getting food from a table in the middle. As soon as they go in he feels exposed, stood there in the bright room for everybody to look at. There is the noise of chairs scraping as people take their places and start eating. Dia is gone ahead into the queue, and Mick joins the end of it, one of the chefs getting in just before him. He stays close behind and shuffles forward. There is a great purple wart on the back of the guy's neck, his skin raw and pink around it where it's been catching his collar. Somebody behind him too now, he can hear him puffing his frustration at the queue. 'Come on, come on.' His eyes on Mick's back, taking him in. Chefs pushing in further up the queue; nobody saying anything.

Here are the eggs, then. By the time Mick gets to the table, eggs is mainly what's left, plus a few sausages, beans, fruit salads. He doesn't care. He just wants to get sat and get eaten, go back to his room.

Dia is on a table of black men, four of them sat together in green overalls. Mick goes to the other row, sitting himself at one end where the seats all around are empty. Further down there is a group of women, all dark haired, foreign-looking. One of them keeks over at him at one point, and he realizes he must be sat where their pals are about to sit. He eats up his breakfast quickly and at random. No that it's a meal you'd want to linger over. One sausage, a slice of bread, and a small clot of beans sharing juices with three pineapple slices. Nay wonder they're all so miserable.

Everyone's in their own group – the baldies at one table, the waiters another, the receptionists – all of them keeping in with themselves. It's like school. And it's so quiet, that's the strangest thing. Hardly anybody talking, just chowing their food down in silence, the only noise in the room the sound of knives and forks hitting plates. Most of them look foreign, maybe that's part of it, the lack of mixing. Still but, who's he to talk, the cloyed-up Scot there at the end of the row.

He is finishing off when the head chef comes in and walks over to him. He stands stooping opposite him, his hands pressed on the table.

'Go okay today?'

'Fine, aye, once I'd got the hang of it.'

Some of the women are looking over.

'You need to get your speed up, that's all.' He stands straight, looking off toward the door, then back at Mick. 'Next staff food is at five, and your late starts at half past, okay?' He pats once on the table and walks away.

He doesn't go to the next staff food. He holes up in his room, laid on the bed in his pants and his socks, done in, drifting in and out of sleep through the afternoon.

The late shift is longer, relentless, more types of crockery. At least but he is in the bare scuddy underneath the overalls, which is a pure blessed relief compared to earlier. And as well he manages to wrestle a few more words out of Dia, who is on with him again.

'Where are ye from?'

'Ghana.'

He realizes it's coming to a close when the waiters are only leaving tea and coffee cups, and these wee pots skinned with leftover mustard and ketchup.

When the kitchen start bringing all their pots and pans through, Dia gives him a hand scrubbing them clean, and afterward shows him where the mop is to follow where he's already swept. They are about done when one of the baldies comes through with a bottle of beer in his hand, sheer-legging over the wet floor to reach for his knife bag off one of the shelves. A beer. That would be pure fucking heaven right now. He doesn't say anything to Dia though, and they finish up, draining the machine and bringing out the rubbish bags before they leave, away back to the staff quarters.

He gets into his room and tummels onto the bed.

19

The next day is much the same; and the next. His body is feeling like it's took a kicking. By the time his day off comes, he's that exhausted it is all he can do to get out of bed in time for staff food, and he spends most of the rest of it asleep.

The rota is two shifts each day out of breakfast, lunch or dinner, and one day off a week. His mind is occupied, near enough, and then when he's no working he's too tired even to think. He gets kept on Wash 1 for the first week, either with Dia or with Eric. He doesn't try getting any patter out of them so it's aye quiet working, but no that it's frosty or anything, it's fine, it's just work. They two have their own reasons they don't yap on, the same as he does, and so they get on with it just, silently working as a team while the baldies flash in and out with hot pans and the waiters gurn through the hatch.

The afternoons, which are only a couple of hours if he's on a lunch, he rests up in his room, or he goes out the back fire exit to the terminal for a pint, or sometimes, if he can't stomach the idea of returning for the lunatic buffet, a sandwich.

The later staff food is harder going even than the breakfast. Usually there's a tray of mince, without tatties, and a tray of carrot omelette, or onion omelette, or sausage omelette. Then it might be chips, which are away in a second, and hard, chewy rice that gets stuck between your teeth. He sits at the correct table now. Takes his place with his African co-workers and chows away silently next to them. He asks the other two their names. Obi and Vincent. They wear the same green overalls, but they work in a different kitchen, he doesn't know where.

One day after the breakfast shift, the head chef comes in the potwash to tell him he needs to go up and see the operations manager: she has to get his details on the system.

He goes after staff food. Her office is on the same level as the kitchen, through a corridor with the same scuffed carpeting and bare walls as the rest of the staff side, but the occasional plastic plant and a wall clock with the hotel logo on it. A few shabby efforts at perking up the gloom – it's in fact no unlike the walk used to be up to Alan's office – which maybe explains how his stomach is feeling right now. Away, it's Mick! Good to see you. You're a kitchen porter now, I hear. Good for you, that's great.

He's about to chap the door, but he hears voices inside, what sounds like an argument, and he hangs back. Hard to make out what they're saying, but it's two women. Probably he should get leaving. But then there is movement inside, and he presses back against the wall as one of the housekeepers comes out, leaves the door open, and is away muttering down the corridor. The operations manager appears, sees him, scowls.

'I'm here to fix out my details.'

She turns away. 'Wait.'

The door shuts, and a few moments later she shouts him to come in.

She gives him a sheet of paper to fill in and ignores him, busy writing quickly onto a pad. She's rattled, clear enough. He can feel the movement in the desk as she writes. A great black printer between them with Post-it notes stuck on it: *Tronc adjustments. Gerry, Plane Food, 4 p.m.*

Scottish, he puts on the form, and Mick; the rest he makes up. He's filling this out on a need-to-know basis, is how it's going to go, and there's fine well certain things they don't need to know. Provan, he calls himself, after Dave Provan who played for Rangers when he was a wean. As he passes the form to her, he says that he doesn't have a bank account. She doesn't try hiding the scunnered expression that comes on her face, but it seems at least she believes him. They'll pay him in cash, she says, until he's got one. An envelope job. Nay problem. Nay problem at all.

When the first paypacket comes, handed to him by the head chef at the start of one dinner shift, he doesn't have any pockets to put the by a long wail. For a moment there is silence but then it comes again, a loud scurling sound. Like a fox; no something human. He closes his eyes, wanting to shut it out, but he can't, even in the quiet in-betweens, because he is braced, the heart tromboning, waiting for it to come again. He inches the bag down from his face and props up onto his elbow to try and see over the hill of whatever he's next to. There is no movement anywhere. Only the dim shapes of all these others, who don't seem to notice this desperate wailing noise, merging it instead into their own nightmares.

A hand on his shoulder. There is activity in the room, voices, light streaming in through the large, high windows. Somebody stood above him; walking away. He lies there rigid and watches as the cocoon next to him squeezes itself out. No a butterfly, that's for certain. He is old and scarred, the hair clotted, deep trenches in his face. Mick doesn't move, watching from inside his bag – all these hopeless creatures stooping and coughing, gathering up their beds. There is one pair that look young enough they could be school-weans. Blacks too, Asians, the whole circus. Yann is there, chatting with a few of the other Hallelujahs, who bring out long tables and unfold them at one side of the hall. Women start appearing. Broken-looking women, worse gone even than the men. He sits there in a stupor taking it in. He's seen plenty enough scaffers before, in book-ies, the park, on the street, but this is something different, seeing them all together in a room. Yann is coming over.

'How did you sleep, Mick? We have breakfast now, so if you want to queue up, they'll have it out in a moment.' A line is already form-ing by a table at the other side of the hall. 'Here.' He hunkers down beside him and hands him a leaflet. 'Each of these churches opens for a different night of the week. You can self-refer to any, but you'll need to book your place first.'

He half listens to the rest of Yann's spiel before joining the back of the queue, behind a woman with no socks on, her baries scarlet and bloated. None of it is registering properly. He sits down where there is nobody next to him. Staff food all over again. Except this is a better meal at least: scrambled egg, bacon, beans. Head down, he eats fast, ravenous and wanting to get out. Somebody is pulling in opposite him but. Mick keeks up, then back to his food. A man in a red woolly hat. His giant bawface blistered and shot, a drinker. If he can just get eaten up, leave this place, no talk to any of them. But this guy is staring at him.

'Ye don't always get the beans, know. Serious, ye don't.'

A bloody Weegie. Unfuckingbelievable. Mick doesn't look up. He resolves no to let a word slip out of his mouth.

'See the bacon is always – ye always get the bacon but the beans is hit and miss. Believe that? I'm telling them, get more beans. Beans is cheaper for them and it fills ye up the better.'

Mick nods, picking up his plate and standing.

He puts the plate and cutlery into the buckets on the table. How can somebody like that look at him and think – aye, there's a guy that's on my wavelength? No point dwelling on it but. Probably a headbanger. He goes warily over to his bag and then makes for the door, getting out the building before any other nutter can clamp onto him.

25

A man in a suit is sitting on a bench. A short way down the towpath, an elderly Mediterranean-looking woman in a huge fur coat is waiting for her small dog to finish shitting beside a tree. The man knows full well that she is not going to clear it up. He knows it, and it is irritating the hell out of him that he knows it, but still he cannot move his eyes away: the dog squeezes out the final pellet, and he watches in silent fury as the woman slowly wanders off in her enormous coat.

The man turns back to his lunch, but that just serves to annoy him further, so he looks up at Battersea Power Station instead – something reassuring about the size and solidity of it. He could kill for a sausage sandwich right now. That was his old routine: after the first couple of weeks last summer when all the new advisers would go together from the Department for Business building to the pub for lunch, he had taken to walking down to the river and buying a sausage sandwich en route. He looks down miserably now at his Boots meal deal: the juice drained in one go, sandwich vanished, colourful delights of the fruit salad still to come. The homeless man is there again. He is sat three benches further up, and there's little chance he could have seen him but even so the memory of yesterday returns, and he experiences for a moment the same sense of panic he had felt as the man had approached him, the crazed look on his face. He seems to be keeping to himself today, ignoring the passers-by and just glaring out at the river in what appears to be the same dirty brown jacket and torn trousers as he had on before.

He attempts the fruit salad. It is dry and soapy; he compresses a piece in his mouth but no moisture comes out. He knows that it is almost time to return to the office, but as soon as he thinks about leaving the bench he starts to become a little nauseous. There is a pre-meet at one to brief the Idiot for his afternoon meetings. No doubt the others will be prepared: they'll have been planning over lunch, devising a briefing strategy. They will have choreographed their spiel; and when, at the end of the brief, the Idiot turns to him and asks if he has any input, he will look every inch the pointless fat fool as he replies that he believes it's all been covered. In his whole time there so far, his single most significant contribution was the moment during a meeting with the Federation of Small Businesses when the Idiot passed him a squiggled note that read: *What is the minimum wage these days?* Remembering the stupid flush of pride that he had experienced on sliding back the answer causes the sick feeling in his stomach to increase now, as he rises from the bench.

A runner comes past in a gold-coloured pair of lycra trousers, his large muscular buttocks seizing as he pounds down the tow-path. The man starts back toward Westminster, but immediately as he does so the strange, horrifying image enters his head of himself in the same pair of trousers, entering the building and suddenly everybody looking at him – the security guards suppressing their mirth as he passes through the scanners – and the sight of his fat golden arse repeated all around him in the unending glass and mirrors and polished flooring. Suddenly he stops right there on the towpath, looking round to check nobody is nearby, and, with the fruit salad punnet, he scoops up the four small nuggets of dog shit from beside the tree. He ties up the Boots carrier bag around it, continuing alongside the river, and drops the package into the next dustbin he passes.

Further down the water, Mick is viewing across the way to the power station. One thing that must be admitted: it's bloody big. When did they close it? Who cares, what does it matter? It doesn't. Probably the Milk Snatcher but. We don't want power stations, what we want instead is more apartment buildings – these ones you can see here all along past the bridge, curving swirls of bright blue and green.

He pulls out the leaflet and turns it over. One thing that's obvious, looking at the map: these churches are spread miles apart. And, on top of that, the Monday one is the other side of the map from Tuesday, which does not neighbour Wednesday, and so on, and so on. Obvious it's done on purpose. To make things difficult, for whatever reason. The absurdity of it all. An absurd situation, would ye no agree, Mr Jogger, in your – and let's be honest here – pretty daft leggings? Fucksake, he needs a drink. The pub just a little way down the road but him sat here with no money on his tail. Cruel. Very cruel.

It takes him two hours to walk there, and he arrives while it is still light. Maybe that's how they keep them so far apart. To give the scaffers something to do. Pass the time. The Hallelujah that comes to the door isn't as friendly as the other one. He's in fact quite annoyed that Mick's turned up out the blue without booking his place. He's not supposed to arrive before seven. He should have phoned ahead. A good one, that. See the thing is I was going to call ahead on the mobile phone but then I was that busy on the line with clients and contractors and all that, I forgot. He doesn't bother arguing with the guy. No the energy or the pride, so he keeps quiet and the man agrees to book him in, only he has to go away the now and no come back until seven o'clock. He leaves, walks about, wondering how he's supposed to know when seven o'clock is.

Shepherd's pie and a spoon of boiled vegetables. The set-up is different here – it's a bigger place, and there are small round tables to sit at, but he manages to find one where he's on his own. He recognizes one or two of the faces. The beans guy is here, sat over the way at a full table, laying it off to some poor ancient scaffer about something or other.

The Hallelujahs wait until everybody has got food, then they fix out plates for themselves and sit down inamongst the tramps. Mick stares down at his plate, eating quickly, but nobody comes. Afterwards he gets a sleeping bag and finds a space, then sits against the wall next to it, making sure he doesn't catch eyes with anybody. Some of the scaffers stand together in dirty clusters, talking. Others keep with themselves, avoiding the groups, like he is doing. No. As long as he remains outside of it, eating the food just and accepting the shelter for now, and no talking to any scaffers or any Hallelujahs, then he will stay afloat. Only if he accepts that he is part of this, that he belongs here, will he be done for. Because if he does that, then there'll be no control over it, and he may as well throw in the towel. Game over.

A dribbly day, but no too cold. He takes a free paper from a stall he passes, to lay down on the bench. Irrational, maybe, no the sensible man's choice, but he goes the trek to his usual spot. The night's church is in the other direction but it doesn't matter, better anyway to use up the day by walking. He is sat staring at the power station when a young lad, looks like a student, comes and sits in next to him. It isn't long before he turns and starts talking. Mick keeps quiet, hoping he'll get the message. He doesn't. Incredible sight, he is saying, wet day, and all this. Go bloody sit inside well if it's too wet for you. He has started fiddling about in his rucksack.

'Would you like a muffin?'

Mick ignores him.

'It's okay. It's spare.' He is holding his muffin out to him. 'Well, I'll just leave it here in case you change your mind.'

The boy stays sitting there. He keeps looking over, Mick can see him doing it out the corner of his eye. After a while, he turns toward the lad, the muffin still there on the bench between them.

'I've ate already. I'd take a pound but, get myself a cup of tea.'

The boy obvious isn't too sure about this and he delays a moment, nay doubt thinking – how do I know he isn't going straight the offie with this? Which is exactly where he intends going with it, but the lad is by now getting out his wallet, and he hands him £1.50.

He uses the money smartly. £1.29 buys him a decent-size bottle of Polish lager and he saves the rest to call ahead to the church. It runs out after about five seconds, but the guy rings him back.

The journey is much more pleasurable with a drink inside him. No bevvied, but warmer, more relaxed. In such a state it is easier to ignore all the rub-ye-ups bustling past and eyeballing him along the pavement. Away home to their evenings of curry dinner and telly watching, argle-bargling with the wife. Plenty of scaffers about too: alone in doorways; stood in wee groups; blocking the thorough-fares selling their magazines. He is coming into a more posh area. There are wine drinkers inside a giant café window, flower stalls, well-to-do clothes shops. This one that he passes. A naked manne-quin in the window, bald and bare, with the one hand on her hip. The sudden temptation to run in and steal her. Run off down the street with the baldy woman tucked under the arm. How far would he get? How many yards down the pavement before the heavy mob catch up, huckling him down some back alley to put the boot on?

No that there are many back alleys this part of town. Nay chance. It's all boulevards and butchers round here, they Italian ones with cured meats hanging in the display above the olive oils and the giant cheese wheels.

It is a Catholic church this night, and the space is a side room off the church building itself, the walls above the sleeping mats covered with ornate lanterns and candles, lifelike statues of nuns holding crosses and looking out with serious faces at the scaffers. There are less staying than the previous two nights, but still one or two of the regulars, they ones that know they're onto a good thing and have got themselves in with the bricks. He ignores them, managing to keep to himself. Eats his food. Drinks his tea. There is a prayer session after dinner, but the Hallelujahs don't force it. Quite a few take part though, going through with the Bead Rattler, who has been walking about the place in his robes and his rings, for a wee patter with the Big Man. Hard to know how they're asking him for anything.

He rolls out his mat and his bag and gets lying down. How quick you get used to things. Settle into a rhythm.

In the morning after breakfast, one of the Hallelujahs, a woman, approaches him.

'Sleep okay?'

'Fine, thanks.'

She stands by the tea table while Mick is fixing up his tea and his orange juice. How is it people are always wanting to put the nose in and can't leave him be?

'It's Mick, isn't it? I haven't met you before. My name's Jenny.'

'Pleased to meet ye, Jenny,' and he starts to turn and get leaving back to his place at the table.

'I was wondering – have you had a chance to use the daytime centre at all?'

'I have, aye, thanks.'

'Oh, right. Good. And you know we have caseworkers too, who can help you with accessing services.' The beans guy is arrived at the table making a tea, listening, a wee smile on him.

'Thanks, Jenny, I'll bear it in mind.'

'Right, okay.' She smiles and starts to move off. 'Have a nice day, Mick.'

Oh, aye, it's going to be a belter: away down the boulevard for a new suit, then off to a restaurant with the baldy woman for Guinness and oysters.

'How's it going?' Beans is looking at him, still the wee grin. The red woolly hat pulled right down to his eyes.

'Good.'

'Ye from Glasgow, well?'

No use kidding on now he's been rumbled.

'I am.'

'Whereabout?'

'Clydebank.'

'That where ye were born?'

'Aye, Clydebank.'

He gives a wide smile. One side of his top lip is chappit and bleeding. 'I'm from Paisley.' He holds out a giant purple hand. 'Keith. Ye're no a religious case, eh?'

'No.'

Beans turns his eyes for an instant up to the roofbeams. There is a large dark gouge in the stubble under his chin. 'Thank Christ for that, then. Enough of them about, no think?'

'The Hallelujahs.'

He lets out a loud lunatic laugh, which makes Jenny and the woman she's with look round a moment. 'Aye, the Hallelujahs, you said it, pal, fucking right.'

He is still chuckling with himself as Mick gets leaving.

Where do they go to? There's aye the ones that are sat in the doorways and selling the magazines, but what about the rest of them, where do they go? The women? You never see the women. The nights at the churches, there's been quite a few of them put up. They get a separate room, or if it's one of the smaller places they get a plastic barricade wheeled up in between to keep the men off them. The tollie tugboat is on the approach, docking up with its cargo of shite. He watches it turn around on the water, coiling slowly into the wharf. No great mystery but. It's pretty obvious where most of them go, the men anyway, the male scaffers. They ones that aren't sat next to a carry-out cup, tapping pedestrians for the price of a bottle, are down the broo office signing on. See but how is he any different? Sponging off the Christians for food and orange juice. Fucksake he eats more than anybody there!

He doesn't stop going. He's there each night for his free meal and his free entertainment, listening to the night terrors erupting through the hall. He has a shapeless awareness that he needs to be doing something, but it's getting more difficult to hold the thought and do anything with it. The brain is unable to deal with it. The Hallelujahs aren't but. They keep going on at him about it. Especially the guy Yann. Does he know there's a laundry and showers at the daytime centre? Has he had any thoughts what he's going to do when the shelters close at the end of February? He's going up to Glasgow, he tells him. Going back to see the family. Yann is delighted. That's good, Mick. That's very good.

What will happen to all this lot then? Where will they go? They're that settled into the routine, some of them. Maybe they are actually in fact secret bloody millionaires and when this all packs up they're away in their jets to their lochside mansions, and that's how they're all so unbothered about it, who knows? Because that's what they are. Unbothered. It's true. Rare there is an incident. Sometimes but. Nothing much. The odd squabble a couple of times, arguments over who's took whose sleeping space, but that's usually it. It is a while before he sees anything like a proper fight, and when he does, it's two women. The one of them starts screaming at the other that she's stole her gloves, and when she denies it and starts walking away, the accuser jumps her from behind and gets clawing at her face. The Hallelujahs are straight in there, breaking them up, wheeling out an extra divider the night.

Beans reckons he knows the whole back story. He is sat down at the same dinner table laying it off to him.

'She's had they gloves for years, see. She was gave them as a present by somebody, so ye can see how she's angry. I'd be angry, somebody lifted my hat. I'd be fucking beeling.' Mick sits drinking his tea. 'Know what I think?' Beans continues. 'I think it's no about the gloves. Probably there never was a pair of gloves even. Sometimes it's like that, know what I mean? Christmas is aye the worst. This place is eggshells then. Depends what like is the family situation, course, but most of these lot are biting the carpets.'

Christmas. He's not even noticed that it has came and went. He must have been at the hotel. He tries to mind when it would have been, if there'd been any sign of it, but he can't think; the whole thing is a fog. Plus as well this great bampot right in his face.

'See me, I'm no staying around much longer.' He is looking intently across the table at Mick.

'How's that?'

'Mean, I know this place, close, quite close, beds, kitchens, comfy, ye know, no like this.' He turns and looks about behind him a moment. 'All I want is to go for a crap in peace.'

He is grinning at his joke. Mick notices there are bits of dandruff on the outside of his hat.

'See how I'm telling ye is because you should go there too, we should both of us go there. Ye can't stay here.'

Mick looks away over to where the tables are getting folded back up for the night. The first of the sleeping mats being rolled out onto the floor. He's right, obviously. The memory then of the pub back-yard, the cold humming generator. At least this guy has got something going on upstairs, unlike himself. He's thinking, at least. Even the headbangers have the march on him these days.

It rains a couple of days solid. Quiet down by the river during this time, the fast-flowing water foaming and stinking with the down-pour. The occasional determined jogger dragging past. It is too wet to stay there. He'll be sat thinking it isn't so bad because the bench is partly covered over by a tree, but then a branch will give up under the gathering weight and dump a bucket onto his head. He goes up the coach station. He sits in the bays, drookit and shivering, frighten-ing the passengers. Pneumonia but, it's good for the handouts. Both days, he taps a pitying face for the price of a can and goes to drink it under the railway bridge, or on the walk over to the night's church.

Beans is sat near the end of a long table, on his own. Mick goes over and sits in opposite him.

'Alright?'

Beans is away with it though, staring down at his untouched chicken and chips.

'What ye said before, mean, I think I might take ye up on the offer.'

Beans looks up slowly. 'Offer.'

'Aye, what ye said, this other place.'

Beans doesn't say anything. He stares off now to the side, at nothing, at the wall. Maybe he's bevvied. He doesn't smell but; no of drink, anyway.

'Well, I thought I'd let ye know, okay.'

He doesn't push it after that, and carries on eating his food while Beans sits there, vacant, until after a while he pushes his chair out and walks off, leaving his food where it is.

Mick watches him, over on the far side of the room, sitting down with his back against the wall. A new one, this. He's never seen him when he hasn't been bouncing off the ceilings and chewing everybody's ear off. He continues staying there, alone, while the tea comes out and then the chairs and tables are cleared away, and he's still there, unmoving, while Mick and the others are getting into their sleeping bags for the night. A Hallelujah goes over to him eventually and he gets up slowly, moving over to his pitch.

The next evening though Beans comes up to him in the car park where Mick is stood waiting for the church doors to open. He does mind the conversation. And no just the first one either, but the no-conversation last night as well.

'So what I thought was Sunday.' There is a scaffer sat smoking on the steps who tilts his head up to listen, and Beans pulls Mick off to the side. 'See the thing is Sunday's a good day to try cause there's always chuck-outs the weekend, after people have been on the batter.'

'I'm no sure, mean it's –'

'Nay worries, I'll sort it, I'll sort it. I know the place, see, I know how to play it.' He grins. 'A bed, man. A fucking bed, eh.'

Hard to know what to think, and hard to think at all anyway, so he doesn't. He sits near Beans at tea and half observes him rattling on ten the dozen to anybody that goes near him. They eat. Go to sleep. Up the next morning and he's out again into the cold, away the long stiff journey to the shelter of the coach station. His feet are pretty swollen getting. The walking, or the temperature, or his socks, which cling now like a second skin. One moment to the next. That is all he can do. One moment to the next. Avoid the Hallelu-jahs and sit quietly as he gets his ear chewed off by this strange creature that is smiling at him now. 'Come on, then.' Plates getting cleared away. 'Ye ready?'

26

'See, what I'm saying is never let them think that ye've hit the scrape because if they do then that's you screwed, man, terrible, fucking terrible. They'll never leave ye alone. Plus as well they'll give ye the worst of everything – room, bed, fire alarm, giro, the whole bag all to shite.'

Mick looks down at the pavement. It is dark. Cold. Their breath fluming in front of them as they walk. Actually, no – Beans's breath fluming in front of them – because he never shuts up. Since they left the church it's been non-stop: benefits, religion, piles, the population of birds. He needs to rest but he's too tired to think about doing anything but trail along with this guy through the dark streets, stumbling into busyness where the pavements are hoaching at bus stops and crossings; down deserted side roads, past closed shops, pubs, a girl with her arms tightly folded, smoking in a doorway. The problem with birds, he is saying, is that they're all dying because the farmers are greedy arabs and they've torn down all the hedgerows, the same as they tear down the tenements and now there's nothing, everything is bare just. Mick is trying no to listen. This place they are going to was supposed to be close by, but they've been walking Christ knows how long and he doesn't recognize any more where they are. To close the eyes just. Close the eyes. Sleep. No have to think. No have to listen.

'Where d'ye say it is, this place?'

'Naw, don't worry, don't worry. It's near here. I know where it is.'

'Ye've stayed before, well?'

Beans halts abruptly on the spot, jolts his body upright. 'Have I stayed before? *Course* I've stayed before. *Course* I have.' And he starts walking again, chuckling to himself. Has he been bevvying? It's hard to tell. He's a mighty queer ticket, whichever way. There is a period of quiet. They keep on. No a slow pace either – the guy walks with these great loundering strides, the shoulders stooped over and hunching, bunching, as he steps. It had came as a surprise, during the lunatic moment back there, how tall he actually is when he stands straight. A big man, and this large army-type overcoat that he wears, making him look even bigger. Impossible but to tell how old he is. The hair, when he's took off the woolly hat to sleep, is a full coverage – dark, straggling below his ears and greasy as drag-chains. His face though, lined and scarred; purple. Whatever it is he's been doing with himself, it looks like he's been doing it a long while.

He is trying now to hoick his tattered Ikea bag higher onto his shoulder. Mick is conscious of his own faded holdall, smart in comparison, and as well his clothes, which if maybe they aren't the cleanest, they are normal clothes, they are his clothes. He isn't going around in an army greatcoat and a pair of silver running trainers with the soles flapping off them. Beans is hammering away again: the weather, how it's freezing but it isnae wet and that's the important thing because it's blashie weather that's the worst. Jesus, he could do with a drink.

'See, look, this is what I'm telling ye. Here.'

They are outside a grey concrete building at one end of a street. A woman's voice on an intercom by a heavy, unmarked door and they are getting buzzed in. A corridor; straight ahead a staircase and two doors off either side. Bare walls and grey carpet tiles. The strong smell of bleach. Beans doesn't seem too sure where to go and he hesitates a moment, a quick neb in the one door, then back out, and he tries the other one; goes inside. Mick follows him in.

It looks like a doctor's waiting room: plastic chairs backed against the walls and a single battered settee, a small television that is turned off, and a low table sprawled with mangled, thick magazines. An Asian woman is sat at a computer on the other side of a small security hatch. Beans goes straight up and puts his hands onto the counter. They look massive in the stark lighting, veined like cabbages.

'We've booked a place the night. I was in earlier.'

Mick sits down on the settee. Comfort flooding his legs. He could go to sleep right here, close the eyes, go to sleep.

'No, see, I came in Sunday but there was no rooms so I was told come back the day and they told me earlier there was places for us, that's what I'm saying.'

The woman's voice is hushed, barely audible past his huge back. He is arguing with her; the protective shutter above the hatch about to roll down any moment. Beans turns then and comes toward the settee. He dumps down and Mick near slides onto his lap.

'Says we've got to wait for the hostel manager. She's no too sure we're booked in but that's pure crap – I was here the morning and I spoke to the guy, I telt him we were coming. Fucking *indirect* access, ye ask me.' He keeps speaking, but Mick sits in a kind of a daze, wanting to let the brainbox go to rest. Hostel. He is in a hostel. He tries no to think about what is happening; trying no to think about any of it, least of all this blowhard sat here next to him, staring now at the underwear models in a worn-out clothing catalogue. An agitated old black man noses in at one point, his trouser bottoms rolled up unevenly to show dirty yellow walking socks. He glances toward the television a moment, then backs out.

Mick is falling asleep, Beans quietly looking at the magazines, and another man coming in, younger, smarter, a trimmed beard. Beans is stood up, talking to him. The man goes away, through a locked door into the room with the woman; returning with sheets of paper. He gives some to Beans, then he's looking down at Mick, handing him the papers and saying something – he can't hear it properly, it's quiet like a radio with the batteries going – benefits, it is something about benefits. He tries to sit up. The man is talking to Beans again. No visitors. No alcohol. No drugs. He repeats it. Beans nodding his head. Grinning. He looks demented.

The room is small. A cubicle. Three beds with high plastic sides, lined up like cots. He puts his bag down at the foot of one of them and looks out the small window at a brightly lit car park. Lies down on the bed. He can hear Beans outside, laying it off to the man because the room isn't big enough. He stares up at the ceiling. The same smell of bleach; sanitizer. Strange but he is glad of Beans being there. The ceiling is starting to swim. He shuts the eyes. So tired it feels his breathing is about to give out.

A shout wakes him. He sits up. His clothes are on and it is dark apart from some lights outside a window. A hollow racing sensation as he gets his bearings. There is another shout; it is in the corridor – *Go on!*

it sounds like. Then feet pounding and a tremor in the floor as they come past his room. *Go on!* More than one person. Three or four. Men's voices. A moment later it is quiet again, but the tight panicked feeling does not leave him and he lies there rigid, exhausted but no able to get back to sleep.

When he wakes up again it is getting light outside. The room is empty. Tummelled sheets on one of the beds. He is hungry, but he doesn't know if there is a breakfast in this place. He doesn't know what or where the place is either, for another thing. After a while he gets up and listens through the door, and goes out.

The kitchen along the corridor is empty. Plates and pans are heaped in the sink and there are blackened scratchings of food littered on top of an electric hob cooker. Something in the room which is boufing. Doesn't smell much like food but, and he realizes as he gets closer that it is the bin. He moves away from it and toward the fridge. Inside, a bundled-up Tesco carrier and a snipped-open packet of pasta sauce inside the door. That's the lot. A stank of yellowish liquid pooled at the bottom. Second inspections but, and he undoes the carrier to find a plastic tub of cocktail sausages. No like they're going to miss a couple, and no like he's fussy either, so he puts one in his mouth; but there is something wrong about the taste of it, and he gets standing up, shuts the fridge door, awful, fucking awful. Posters on a noticeboard. Needle exchange. Substance-use worker. His stomach lurches and he bends over the sink, about to boak, but he doesn't – he stays there, poised, with the stomach spasming but nothing coming up, just this thin dribble hanging off his lip. He sticks the tap on and swills his mouth. The rush of water splashing against the plates and pans and wetting his front. Where is he? He wants suddenly to laugh. Where in fuck is he? He turns off the tap and goes out, back to the empty room, and into the bed.

Beans is stood at the foot of the bed, looking at him.

'Fancy getting some breakfast eh?'

Mick gets up automatically, without thinking. Starts putting his shoes on. Beans is over by the window, his hands clasped behind his back, calmly gazing out as if it's a loch view.

Once outside, they are straight away on the march. No the worst day. Warm on those parts of the pavement that the sun is shining, although pretty snappy still in the shaded areas, past offices and residential blocks, under a bridge, past a line of parked buses. They go by a small scrub of a square and a mob of scaffers around the benches on one side. Seven or eight of them, women in the mix, sitting and standing about, drinking. Beans slows down, watching them. For a moment Mick is feart he is wanting to go over, but they carry on past, although Beans still has his attention turned to the group. They continue up the way. Truth is, he's glad to be out of the hostel. Away from that room. Probably most of that group back there are staying in the place too. The thought of it, of being in there with them, himself in a room alongside, it doesn't make sense. He can't reckon with it. Better outside in the open, away from it, even if that means being with your man here. They are stopped outside a cafe. A large scratched sticker on the window – a fat chef holding up a steaming forked sausage. Beans is going in, but Mick hesitates outside.

'Ye coming in?'

'Aye.' But he stays where he is, looking in past the fat chef.

Beans grins. 'It's on me, pal, it's on me, don't worry.'

'No. It's no the game,' but Beans is off inside already, and he follows him in.

They go up the counter and Beans immediately orders two breakfasts and two teas, then they get themselves sat at a table by a wall, away from the busy middle of the room. Pathetic. He knows it is. Somehow but he can't feel it. He's that hungry, and weak – that's what it is, a weakness – that he can't bring himself to say no. The breakfasts come and Beans is beasted right in, mushrooms flying about, ketchup and brown sauce and mustard all mixed together on his plate like a mental sunset. Every bastard in the place probably looking at them. The odd couple in the corner. It's a good breakfast though. A buttery stack of toast, the warm mush of the sausage. Suddenly the thought that maybe Beans doesn't have the money to pay for it either, and he's going to do a run-out. The scunnered faces of the other customers and the cafe owner on the phone to the polis.

He does have the money, it turns out. A ten-pound note comes out the pocket, calm as anything, no chicanery, no hysphericals. He walks up the counter just, pays, and they leave.

It is bright out still. They walk for quite a while, Beans talking – they aren't allowed back into the hostel while evening, he is saying – until they arrive, suddenly, at the river. A stretch he doesn't recognize. Beans is saying he wants to show him something, and they go through a gate with a broken padlock – *Permits required to access this property for the purpose of nature conservation or fishing* – into a small wooded, weeded area. Down a sloping thicket and thorns path, long grass and random rubbish – empty cement bags, a broken office chair on its side – to a sprawling bush, which they crawl under, emerging onto a patch of open ground that looks out on the water.

'The veranda,' he declares. They sit down, legs dangling over the banking. He likes to sit here and watch the boats and that come past, he says. And to drink too, judging by all the cans lying about. There is a swan who stays under the scrub off to one side where the banking stops, Beans tells him, only she's no there the now because she's out and about getting her nest together. It's hard to believe him – anything he says – but then Mick sees the nest, lower down, sticking out from under the scrub, all these twigs twined into a great bowl on the wet ground amongst plastic bottles and lager cans. Bold as ye like. He gives a smile at the sight of it. These swans that he minds, who made their nests by the fitting-out berths, their feathers clatty with oil, but who'd come and go like they were boating on Loch Lomond.

At one point during the afternoon Beans goes off for a while, and returns with a couple of four-packs. They sit in the sun drinking, and Mick tells him what type are a couple of the boats that come by, Beans listening as if it's the most fascinating thing he's ever heard.

It is only when it gets evening and they are on the approach to the hostel that it starts to loom over him again. The bare room. Bogging of bleach. Surrounded by homeless. They walk past a bar and he almost asks Beans if he fancies going a pint, but obviously it's impossible because of the money situation. It's bad enough he's tapped him already for his breakfast, plus now the cans. So they go in, Beans away into the reception to chin the staff and leaving Mick to go up on his own.

He is on the stairhead about to turn onto the corridor, but there is noise up the way. Voices. He waits round the corner, the heart going mental already. Hard to hear what they are saying, but it sounds like there's a few of them, and this other noise as well that sounds like somebody thumping rhythmically against the wall. He is that fixed on what's ahead of him, he doesn't notice the group coming up the stair behind.

One of them laughs.

'You alright there, mate?'

He spins round. There are three of them. Young lads. They stand there grinning and leering at him.

'Fine, aye,' and he moves on down the corridor, the others up ahead turning to watch him, and these behind following him, one of them making a tootling noise, like a trumpet. He gets into the room, closes the door and pushes one of the cots up against it.

The sun straining a thin light through the curtain. Beans asleep in his clothes. Noises coming and going outside, keeping him awake, on edge.

It is dark. He has been dreaming. Christmas. Christmases, all jumbled together. The first one he is sat in the living room and the boys and the Highlanders are there sat in their positions, a wee plastic Christmas tree behind the television, Lynn sat on the settee next to Alan with her crabbit face on, like it's the last place in the world she wants to be the now, this craphole, with its stained carpets and cramped corridors, and the wobbling banister as he goes up the stair and into the bedroom. Robbie and Craig sat on the kitchen chairs with plates of Christmas dinner on their laps, looking toward the shape in the bed. Craig cutting up the turkey breast into tiny pieces; quartering the Brussels sprouts.

He is awake. The mind out of its box, spinning, all over the place. A few minutes and he's managed to calm himself a little, lying awake until he is able to sleep again.

Another Christmas. Australia. He is sat at the table waiting for her to come in from the kitchen. The cracker hat clamming to his forehead and the full works there on the plate in front of him – turkey, roast tatties and parsnips, bread pudding, cranberry sauce – and outside, all of the gardens down the road are empty because the whole of the Tartan Terrace is at the same game: the only weekend of the summer nobody's got the barbecue out.

Morning, and he's lying in the bed, the body aching, sticking. Beans suddenly in through the door and frowning. He looks at him a moment. 'Breakfast?'

They sit at the same table, the same positions. The only difference is that Beans isn't as rosy this morning: his back is up from something that's happened in the hostel, and it's making him mutter and scratch fork points through his swirly sauce sunsets.

'See the problem is with these people, they've no respect for a person's privacy, know? Mean, it's no better than the clink, serious, and I'm expecting a bit of privacy myself. That's the least I'm expecting.'

'What happened?'

The eyes widen, far enough to expose the white outsider parts that are normally sheltered under the lids. 'What happened? That bastard the manager, that's what. He says to me, the magazines are supposed to stay in the reception, they're no for taking out. Believe that? He's no even asked me. He's telt me I've got them but he's no even asked me first, that's how I'm beeling about it.'

He cloys up then and they don't talk any more about it. They finish eating and Beans pays.

It is colder, blowier, the day, and after a walkabout they go into a train station, park themselves on some seats by a pasty shop. There is a scaffer hanging about the ticket machines and Beans is watching him, the bristles up, like a dog. The smell of pasties wafting; a rare moment of enjoyment. He thinks for a moment how the shame of leeching like this should be making him the more desperate to get doing something, but it's not, it's the opposite – he doesn't think, doesn't care; he is into the routine. They are walking again. Fine but. Fine. Keeping on the move. A stop at the offie on the way to the veranda, and it is okay once they are sat down because the wind is mainly kept off by the bush all afternoon. As soon as they get leaving though, the familiar feeling starts to kick in, the nerves already on edge.

Fortunately but Beans doesn't go in the reception, he's wiped his hands with them, he says, and there is nobody about as they go up the stair and into the corridor. Open the door and go inside the room.

'Aw, Christ.'

It has been turned over. All the bedding is thrown on the floor and the drawers under the one small table are wrenched open. Their two bags have been taken. He sits down heavily on the bed, his breath constricting. Beans is away out the door. 'Fucksake, man. Fucking hell.' He puts his head down on the mattress. Stares out the window. A wean is kicking a ball against the car park wall. He lies listening to it beat repeatedly on the brick.

'She says there's nothing they can do, we should've locked the door. Bastards. Probably them that did it. Serious. It probably was. Ye okay, pal?' A hand is on his shoulder. 'Look, nay worries. No like we had much anyway eh? First thing we'll do the morning, we'll get out of this place. Okay?' He is hauling one of the cots up against the door. 'The better on our own, serious, nay cunts nebbing about.'

27

The group have been there all morning. At any one time there are between four and eight of them: sometimes a pair will wander off toward the street, or a new arrival will come into the square and for a few minutes the silence is broken as the others get on their feet, talking, shouting. One of the women keeps herself slightly removed, on the end bench. If one of the men approaches where she is, starts saying something to her, she ignores him, and eventually he returns to the others. The air of the group is edgy, quiet, getting worse as the morning goes on. Nothing to drink. She feels cold and nervous, sober, aware of the staring line of people at the bus stop.

Shortly before midday, three men arrive, two of them each holding a heavy plastic bottle of cider. The mood changes straight away. There is laughter and movement, the first of the bottles getting opened and passed around. She stays where she is on the bench, and before long another woman comes and sits next to her, passing her the second bottle. This other woman is grinning, looking at her coat. 'Jesus, Anna, alright for some.'

From the first swallow she is elsewhere. Her fear leaving; warmth spreading from deep inside her; the people at the bus stop disappearing. There is a burst of laughter from the group, one of the men saying something that she cannot hear, and the other woman resting her head now against the arm of her coat, closing her eyes. The woman's hair is thin, and she can see there is a rash on part of her scalp, and on the very top of her head, a large dark blue scab.

A fight has broken out. It came out of nowhere – she didn't see what started it – but two of the men are stalking stiffly around each other, and suddenly one of them crumples to the ground as he is struck by something from behind. In an instant the square is filled with shouting, the others in the group rushing in to join the scuffle.

She lifts the woman's head from her arm, lowers it gently to the bench slats and hurries away.

She breathes thinly as she moves down the street, past a line of parked buses and under a bridge, before slowing, her legs aching and frozen. At least her top half is warm. The coat is expensive and new, with a soft lining, and she pulls it tightly around her, making sure that the top is buttoned up to the neck. She needs to pee, but it is quite a way still to where she's headed, so she takes a detour to a public toilet by the river. When she gets there though, she finds it has been boarded up. Fuckers. She is reminded of the stupid drunk dickheads fighting up at the square and she vows not to return there later in the day, whatever happens.

There is a pub on her way and she goes into it. On entering through the heavy swing doors she is immediately watched by the bar girl, and by the time she has gone down the narrow spiral staircase into a dingy basement corridor, there is a large man in chef trousers standing in front of the toilet entrance. He is slowly shaking his head. She turns, avoiding looking at his face, and goes back up the spiral staircase. She walks through the bar; the girl looking at her from behind the counter. Her limbs are heavy and she thinks for a moment that the swing door is not going to open. She desperately needs to pee. With a painful heave the door pushes open, and she turns her head back as she steps through it.

'Fucking bitch.'

There is at least ten minutes left of the journey and she feels like she is about to piss herself. She comes to a side street leading toward a train station and goes down it, crouching behind one of the cars parked next to a high metal fence. Before she has finished, a man, and then a woman with a young teenage girl, come out of the train station exit and start walking along the pavement on the other side of the street. The woman and the girl are talking and do not see her, but the man crosses the street a short way ahead and must see the urine dribbling into the road, because he looks now through the car window at her and for an instant his mouth opens and he mutters something before hurrying away.

When she arrives at the house her mouth feels dry and her arms and legs are faintly shaking as she reaches for the buzzer. She waits in the doorway, until a moment later a man's voice answers, and there is a click as the door unlocks and she lets herself in.

On the veranda, looking out. A yacht coming past, sails blustering in the wind. A woman's face in a porthole. Away to the Med, says Beans. Champagne and Charlie. Only watch out for the Bay of Biscay or ye'll be boaking it all up into the sea. Anyone's guess how he thinks he knows these things. Maybe he does. The money is finished, he says then, but it's nay worry. He's got a plan. He is kneeling up and lifting the bush to get out. Okay? Okay?

There is a noise up on the pavement. A woman's voice, and, quieter, a man's. He tries to listen, no able to pick out the words, but they are getting closer. A gust of wind or something and suddenly he can hear them coming toward him and he scrapes deep into the bush, lying flat underneath it. He cannot let them see him; he pulls his jacket over his head. But they keep coming – they are onto the path now, and he can see the crabbit face, irritated at all these roots and thorns snarling about her ankles. They spot him then, laid out under the bush. She's pure scunnered at the sight of it, but he has a wee smile on him, unsurprised, keeking down now at the cans by his feet.

It is colder when Beans returns, the river turned black and treacly. He has a dark blue ski-jacket-type overcoat under his arm, and a carrier that he starts pulling things out from: a loaf of bread, an open tin of beans, a stack of beers. He sits down next to him. 'Here,' he says, and lobs the coat over. 'Put this over your jacket. Keep ye warmer.'

They make cold beans pieces out of the first few bread slices, and start on the cans. He has been drinking already, it seems. He isn't out the game, but he's talking loudly, laughing, and he makes them clink cans every couple of minutes – plus, each time, an extra one for the swan. 'Thanks,' Mick says, after one of these toasts, 'the coat and that.'

'Aw, you're welcome.' Beans puts on a panloaf English accent.

'You're very welcome.' He takes a long gulp. 'This fella I know, I called in a favour. He's alright, no a bad guy. He's a cunt, ye know, but he's alright.' They are laughing. A warm enclosed feeling from the beer.

'It because I'm from Glasgow, how ye're helping me out?'

'What!' He sits bolt upright and gets standing stumbling to his feet. 'Ye're from Glasgow? Serious? I'd have gave ye the swerve if I'd known,' and he collapses to the ground again, cackling to himself.

In a moment, Beans kneels up. He gets scrabbling feet first under the bush, thorns pulling at his coat and revealing his back, pale and mealy as a white pudding. His head appears over the top of the bush. 'Come on, I'll show ye.'

They go at an angle from the path, through the weeds and the undergrowth, until Beans stops beside some wire netting. An orange sign on it he can't read in the dark. Some kind of a tunnel underneath the road. Beans peels the wiring back and squeezes himself in behind, the wire springing back to its original position. 'Come on.' He steps forward. An old trainer shoe by his feet.

He gets in behind the wiring and it is dark. A smell of stagnant water. Beans is dragging a piece of matting along the ground. 'Here, lie down.' Bits of rock poking at him, their two backs pressed together, shuffling; warm but, where they are touching. The echoing sound of traffic above their heads and the matting no big enough for both their bodies, part of his leg and his arm sticking out and pressing into stones, rubble. The drink but, it is keeping him outside of it, no fully aware, helping him fall to sleep.

Light. The head pounding. His throat dry, chappit, and his legs and his body senseless, except for a jabbing in the small of his back where Beans's elbow is sticking into him. He tries to go back to sleep, but it is too cold and he can't, so he sits up and looks about him. On one side, through the wire, weeds and trees; a glimpse of the dark straining river. There are bits of wood and breezeblocks in the gloom of the tunnel. Dark water pooled into a stank, a Sprite bottle floating on top. On the other side, more wiring, and past it, a construction site – a great hole in the ground, scaffolding, a mini JCB. Beans is sat up now too. Silent. They stay the both of them like that, sitting, for quite a while, and he wonders if maybe Beans is hungover, that's how he's no talking. But he keeps quiet and to himself into the morning, as they go and sit out on the veranda, cold, shivering, until eventually Beans gets up just, no a word, and leaves.

There is a key ring in one of the coat pockets. *London*, it says on it. A pair of palace guardsmen with their daftie hats on. He turns it about in his fingers. No key. Course not. Why would there be? There must have been once but. Or at least somebody's bought it that had one. A car owner. House owner. Seems unlikely Beans knows a person like that. More likely the coat's been lifted. Nay fucking chance he's taking it off though. He is shaking with the cold now. A bit of a wind and a spray coming off the river. An agity feeling is building, uncertain if Beans is going to bring any drink back this time. He can't bring himself to think about how it will be if he doesn't. A whole day and a night to get through in the cold, time not moving on, clotting around him. He finds a few loose pieces of chinex in the other pocket, puts one in his mouth and chews away.

It is dark when Beans returns. Another half-loaf with him. No beers but. Mick doesn't say anything, and they get eating the bread. He's still in the same mood, Beans, keeping cloyed up, and Mick starts feeling an irritation build inside him that he is behaving like this. He doesn't say anything though. He lets it stay there, choking any words he might get saying, watching Beans chuck the empty loaf packet out onto the water. Sleep is impossible the night. The temperature feels like it's dipped even further. The only warmth, Beans's back sweating against his. He wants to get up and walk away somewhere, just walk, but he can't, he can't move.

Afternoon. The dull anxiety waiting for if there's beer or if there's no beer. There is. A big plastic bottle of superlager. Beans in a good mood too. They get stuck in and numbness starts to flood through him. A distant laugh, which he realizes is Beans. How is he getting it? He'd said the money was gone. He can't be bothered maundering on it but – so what, just drink, just fucking drink it down. He starts laughing. He's like a wee bird. That's what he is. A wee chick, a wee sparrow chick staying put in the nest all day while Beans goes back and forth, getting him food and drink, coming back onto the veranda and regurgitating it up for him. Every day. How many? How many days? Fuck knows, and he is laughing again. He turns round and Beans is laughing too, anybody's guess what at. Strange how the time goes. There it is, stretching out in front of you – only the river, boats, the sound of traffic, and the thought mob raring to stick the boot on.

28

Beans's voice up the path, coming back, talking to himself. The heart starts going, in anticipation, or panic, or habit just, fuck knows. He turns round and looks through the bush, and Beans is there with another man. Panic tightens through him. They are crawling under the bush. 'See here's the guy I'm telling ye about.' The man is nodding at him, sitting himself down on the veranda. He is younger, the hair closely cut, his sweater and his jeans pretty clean-looking. A bottle of superlager is being passed between Beans and the guy, who takes a long pull, gulping twice. Then they pass it to him. The two of them talking. 'They're taking all the old spots, is the problem.' He is English. 'Come over for the building jobs and all that but then they get here and they've already filled all the fucking jobs, so they're out on their arse but they can't afford the fucking fare home.' Beans laughs with him, passing the drink. Then the guy sees the swan and he's off down the banking. A big stick suddenly in his hand and he is laughing, poking it at the nest. The swan is hissing and it's looking like she's going to up and stiffen him any minute, until Beans gets in there first. He jumps on the guy's back and the pair of them start tummelling about in the wet scrub by the nest. Beans on top now, pounding him. Seconds later the guy gets scrabbling up onto the banking and he's away under the bush. 'Fuck are you doing? It's a joke, Jesus, it's a fucking joke.'

He opens his eyes. Daylight. He is outside, and he is freezing. Beans is sat staring out, eating. Mick sits up and he gets handed a sandwich out of a carrier.

He looks at it a moment. 'There's a bite mark in this.'

Beans turns, frowning. 'Aye, so what?'

'Just, mean, there's more teeth marks in it than you've got teeth,' he grins, and Beans creases over, knotting himself.

Later, and Beans is stood above him, giving him these wee kicks in the thigh. 'Come on. We need to go the messages. I told ye.'

Onto the road, the pavements. Odd. Like he's there but he's in fact no there. They are looking at him, but from somewhere else, another consciousness, another world. Like being bevvied. Operating in your own space and everybody else fogging up around the edges of it. No that he's drunk but. The soreness all over his body is sure enough sign of that. 'This is the best time. Ye have to wait the last minute, when the fella's there with his gun, stickering all the stuff up.' True enough, there he is. Fridges. Shopping trolleys. 'Discreet, right. We need to be discreet.' But Mick is started laughing. Discreet! No likely. They look like a pair of cartoon characters, stalking behind tailing the guy as he is going about putting on the stickers. Into the baking aisle. The comforting smell of it. A wean stood staring while his maw chooses between the brown breads. He doesn't know what to make of the pair of them, his mouth in a wee study, slightly open, then he's darting off with his mammy, holding the hand. Beans has a stick of bread, and a piled handful of tinned salmon – *Reduced to clear.*

Outside, in the car park at the back of the building, there is a gap through to where the warehouse bit is. The shutters are closed but up against them there is a stack of red plastic crates. 'Here.' Beans passes him a couple. They are shallow but long and wide, and they have to hold them with arms stretched out, leaving quickly away down the road, taking up half the pavement between them.

'Bread crates,' he says. 'Good mattresses. Plenty of give, see, and they keep ye off the ground.' He's right too. They work well, slotted together with the matting laid out on top, and he is much more comfortable the night, no forgetting as well the bottle of superlager they got from the offie on the way back. He is able to sleep, even though he wakes up often. Each time he does, the tunnel boufing with a rank smell. The sour stankwater – but then there is a hiss of air from behind him, tickling the backs of his legs. The salmon.

Rain. They keep to the tunnel but it is filling up with water, so thank Christ for the bread crates. They stay sat or lying on top of them all night and all day as the blashie weather continues; his body aching, disintegrating, but always auld Beans there, trusty as ever with the bottle. The sun appearing. Beautiful spring sunshine. Daffodils. Bloody daffodils, where they come from? We have received a number of complaints. Sat throwing chuckies into the river, aiming at a can caught up in the yellow foam. Beans is a fair aim. A man of surprises, ye are. Aw, fuck off, pal, I used to play cricket for Scotland, ye know. The pair of them falling about pishing themselves. They are just stood there looking. A few residents have made complaints. Residents? Ye kidding? Who's that, well, the fucking swan? She's fine, man, she knows the score, she's no a bastard like yous. But they aren't finding it so funny, they're just stood there in their high-vis jackets and their fishermen's wading boots. If you don't move, we will have to get the police. Eh, what? Who are yous, then, if you're no the polis? They are laughing again and started throwing the chuckies at these three but the game's over. Up in the air. Suddenly the polis, the protectors of the residents, are arrived and they are being pulled about and corkscrewed up the path – bloody hell, says the one of them, as he keeks the drinks cabinet. They let go of their arms a way up the pavement, and it looks a banker they're about to get slung in the meat wagon, but no – get walking, they are told. The polis following at a short distance behind. Onto the roads and they keep going, miles and miles, turning round one point and the polis are gone, Beans muttering to himself, grumbling, chapping now on a door. After a while an Asian guy opening. No, he says, and he shuts it again.

They are going up a stairwell and his legs give out. He slumps down on the step and Beans is dragging at him until he gets up and labours on. Another door.

'You.'

'Me, aye.'

They are being let in and they follow the backs of a man's legs up a staircase. Who's he? My pal, that's who. A small room and a TV going. He is sitting down on a settee and Beans and the man have went into another room. A plate on the floor with the remains of a jacket tattie, just the well-fired parts of the shell left over. Beans and the man appear in the doorway, grim-faced.

Cans coming out; he gets handed one. The man's eyes are large and swollen, the top lids delicately folded scrotums. The air clung with smoke as he gets through his pack of fags, Beans smoking as well, dog-ends on the floor, a shoe, some bundled sheets. He doesn't say much, your mate, through the smoke. He's fine, he's fine. Darkness, and he wakes, alarmed and shaking. Beans on the settee, one cadaver leg hanging off the edge. He is lying on the floor. The stink of smoke in the carpet. The tattie still there; he crawls over and starts into it, tearing at the boot leather skin.

Always with Beans he's on the march somewhere, some plan or other he's got in his head and he isn't stopping until he gets there. They arrive at a small car park behind a low, flat-roofed building. There is a fence all round with a neat bed of green shoots in front. BUTTERFIELD MEDICAL PRACTICE, on a sign plugged into the soil. Alarm seizes suddenly in his stomach, working up into his throat until he is almost breathless, choking, needing to sit down on the path by the flower bed. Beans slapping him on the back. A pure desperate urge to drink now has hold of him as Beans makes him stand up, and they get walking, away again onto the street.

They come to a park – no a park but more a patch in between a couple of road crossings, with a square of grass and a rubber-matted play area big enough for about three weans a time to go on. A seesaw. A wee elephant slide with a trunk for a chute. There is a bin beside a bench, which Beans has a neb through before going in his pocket and handing Mick a five-pound note. 'Gonnae go the offie while I find us something to eat?'

The man in the offie is a bastard, but what can you do? Mick thumps the two bottles of superlager onto the counter and the guy doesn't say a word, he gives this wee look just, but he's made himself fine well clear enough. I, the seller of refreshments, know that you, the scaffer, are going to get yourself paralytic, and if it so happens that you kill yourself falling into the road, or you kill somebody else falling into the road, then it's no my fault, and I'll stand here with my face to vinegar just to show who is the better out of the two of us. Nay problem. Fine. Just hand over the beer, pal.

29

A woman, coming toward them.

'Excuse me.'

Beans straightening up, the eyes alert suddenly.

'Nay bother, madam. Ye haven't interrupted anything.'

Her hands on her hips.

'You can't drink here. There's kids playing.'

How old is she? Thirty? Forty? Her weans over on the see-saw, and another woman there too, nervous wee looks up the way. Beans is giggling, saying something, impossible to tell what. The woman stood with her arms folded. 'Excuse me.' She is looking at him now. 'Can you understand me?' The weans are stopped playing, lined up on the rubber play area watching. He has a dim sense of wanting her to stay there, a sort of longing, but Beans is acting it still, muttering on, and she is gone, angrily gathering up bags and weans and marching out of the park to go fetch the heavy team, or the polis, or the council – wading boots on, lads, the residents arenae happy.

There is only one bench in the park, so they take turns, a night each, to sleep on it. The nights it isn't their turn they lie out on the grass aside or underneath it. One time but Beans gives a try sleeping on the slide, although it's obvious no big enough, and Mick finds him in the morning crumpled at the bottom of the chute, looking like something the elephant's boaked up during the night.

He wakes. The sour taste of alcohol in his mouth. Against his face is an empty creased bottle that he'd put there as a pillow. The sun is up, and warm already, but he has got the shakes. No just the arms, or the legs, but the whole of him: head, chest, elbows and hips, all the way down to his toes. Shuddering. He caulks the eyes shut but they pinball in the sockets until they are pure throbbing and he can no longer stop this fear that is rising up him, overwhelming him, a genuine terror made all the worse because there is nothing to fix it to, no reason, it is there just. He presses his forehead hard against the slats of the bench, pushing against the ache. Slitting the eyes open. Beans isn't there. The sudden thought but of getting up to look for him – it's impossible, even the thought is impossible and makes his stomach start to heave and his throat retch, even sitting up, even opening his eyes fully, impossible, impossible. Easier to lie there just, shivering and sweating. The sun no helping matters either – sapping him and making him the more nauseous. He hasn't the energy to take off his coat though. The smallest things. Impossible. But through it all he is craving for a drink. An urging of the body; a pure physical need for it, just to stop all this, drive away again the ache and the fear.

It is getting darker and he is cold. Beans has gone for a crap in the bushes beyond the play area. Away on the road, a streetlamp flickering on. Then another. All along the side of the park they are coming on at random intervals, and he realizes that it's the ones in the darkest spots where the smaller trees are coming to leaf which are turning on first. Interesting. The wee things you notice.

Beans is shaking him on the shoulder.
    'Come on, gonnae wake up?'
    'What?'
    'Breakfast.' The familiar grin. His breakfast grin. 'I've been researching.'
    He gets himself up off the ground. It is drizzling and his back is soaked, some of it sweat probably, although he doesn't feel too bad this morning. Their money has ran out, so they haven't drunk the full bucket the last couple of days. They get walking through the rain until a short while later they arrive at a building that looks at first like an office block, but when they go through the glass doors and bare lobby it opens into a large hall, full of scaffers. Bright overhead lights, tables, din. Beans turns to him: 'Ye okay? Check the food, eh. No bad.' He can't see any food. The place is hoaching with scaffers, shuffling about, yapping, staring. 'Ye coming?' Beans is gone ahead and he hurries after him, clinging behind like a wean,

he's that dependent. See what if Beans leaves him? Gets so sick of him laggered onto his back like some diseased lump that he gives him the slip? The possibility of it makes him start to panic as he follows on to a trestle table with large pots of food on it. He waits in behind Beans, copies how he gets his meal and moves to the next area for a tea. They sit down at an empty table and eat hungrily. Toast. Scrambled eggs. 'Pretty good, eh? I should've minded this place earlier. It's one of the best. Only open a couple of hours but, so ye have to be quick.'

A young guy is watching them. He is sat at another table with a couple of others, forking egg into his mouth but clear enough looking over. Beans doesn't seem to notice, or else he's ignoring it. Mick keeks away. He wants to be out of here. Beans has other ideas though: 'Finish this and we'll go the showers, okay?'

In another room there are washing and drying machines, and cardboard boxes full of clothes. Beans is off through a doorway and he is left stood there unsure what to do. An old woman with a name badge hung around her neck comes up and tells him to help himself to some of the clothes, so he rummles through and pulls out a faded black pair of trackie bottoms and a grey shirt with a dark smudge on the collar.

In the next room, through a door marked MEN, there is a queue for showers, and Beans is further up the way already. They aren't communal, thank Christ: there's five or six separate ones, each with a curtain, though a couple of the men at the front are down to their pants already. Fucking terrible, the state of them. Scars and veins and jaundice.

He waits until he is inside a cubicle before he starts to undress. Even removing his coat feels odd. He's no took it off since Beans gave it him. Then he peels off the rest, all of it damp and rotten, clabbered to his skin, and he gets in the shower. It's been that long since he's seen himself in the scuddy that he doesn't recognize himself. As if the body isn't his; it belongs to another time when nakedness was something that had to be dealt with on a daily basis, and now he doesn't own it – he's removed himself from his body like he has from everything else. The only clue that it's there the now: that it hurts. There are bruises on his legs, down his front, his hips, fucking everywhere. His forearm skin is turned loose and chickeny; he pulls on it, the spring gone. The penis down there. Genuine difficult to believe that is his. He puts a hand around it, tries to mind what it means, the having of a penis. Nothing's doing but. His dobber's no sure about it either, and the two of them dither there for a while, waiting for something to happen, a connection. There is none. Or maybe it's just that neither of them are too comfortable about the line of half-naked scaffers queuing outside, which is in fact fair enough, being honest.

He gives himself a good wash, using the soap from the dispenser to rub over his head and his body, and special attention to the feet, which are started looking like a couple of raw beef kidneys. It feels good. The force of the water. Cleaning. Paying attention to all these parts that he's forgot about. The belly button. Armpits. Nipples, christsake.

When he comes out, he goes in the toilets and takes a very satisfying crap. The first time in a long while he's no had to sneak into a pub for one, or go in the park with a stolen toilet roll.

He puts his dirty clothes in a washer. Pretty pleased as well with these new ones. The shirt is a decent fit, and the trousers comfy enough around the waist, even if they are a wee bit on the short side. No the less, see even if his socks are on show, he definitely doesn't look half as daft as Beans does. He clocks him out in the hall and goes toward him, chuckling.

'Jesus. Check you.'

He is wearing a pair of black jeans and a white denim jacket, the both of them a fair few sizes too small for him. Beans grins. 'Gallus, eh?' Then he holds a finger in the air and spins around slowly, showing the back: ATLANTA HAWKS.

'If you say so, pal. If you say so.'

Beans goes back to the clothing room, saying that he forgot to look for another pair of socks, and Mick moves over to the juice table. There are plenty of name-badge people milling about, topping up cups, handing out leaflets, chatting. They don't seem like Hallelujahs. Any case, there isn't anything religious on the walls, only posters everywhere – chiropodist, walk-in clinic, housing advice – things he should be finding out about, probably, but the awareness of it only makes him feel the more sluggish. Through in the clothes room he can see Beans talking to somebody. He is pointing a thumb at his jacket, showing it off, but suddenly a hand shoots out from behind the door frame and grabs him by the collar, pulling him forwards. Beans stumbling, out of sight. There is too much noise in the hall to hear what is going on. He moves quickly toward the room, a few looking in now.

It is the young guy that had been staring. He is stood right up to Beans, putting the face on him.

'Fucking give it me.'

Another guy as well, behind him, eyeballing Beans, who is rocking on his feet, confused. 'Look, see I got it out the box, that's what I –' but he is getting shoved again, the veins on the guy's neck standing out and Beans falling to the floor, straight onto his arse. Mick rushes forward, standing in front of him before the guy can stick the boot on. 'Leave it, come on. What ye doing? Leave it.' The young guy is looking at him, this odd smile, like he knows him.

'The jacket's mine.'

Name-badge men are coming in the door. Beans behind him, getting up. The situation as it is, he looks even more ridiculous right now in the tight denims. The guy's pal is pulling on his shoulder – 'Come on, let's go' – but he's a fair solid build and he's no budging, and it's pretty obvious that the jacket cannot be his because it's way too small for him. In an instant the two men are barging out the room, pushing past the name badges, and it is over, just like that. Beans looks shook up. He is fairly shook up himself; but, through it, a small feeling of elation.

Nobody is moving, and it's Beans who is the first to speak, looking out the door through the bodies. 'Psychies,' he says, going over to the box and starting to root about, still after his socks.

On the way back to the park, carrying a new blanket and their cleaned clothes in carriers, Beans doesn't talk about what has just went on. He patters on as normal, like nothing's happened, telling him instead about the holidays he went on as a wean. Mick has the incident on his mind but. Wondering if Beans noticed his part in it even. 'Fair Fortnight, ye mind it? We'd go to Rothesay. Always there, nay discussions. One time my maw says let's go someplace different

190

this year, maybe go see her cousins and that in Irvine, but the da he tells her we're going to Rothesay and that's that.'

Mick smiles. 'That's where we went, ye know, Rothesay.'

Beans stops in his tracks and a man on his mobile phone almost walks into him.

'Fuck off, serious?'

'We did, aye. Every Fair, mostly.'

Beans is still rooted to the pavement, amazed. Residents diverting past them. 'Mind that station the Friday morning? The platform mobbed with all these Fair Invaders packing in and the conductors playing hell with ye if ye got too close the edge – but what could ye do, eh? There was nowhere else to go!' He starts chuckling. 'Who ye go with, the parents, brothersisters?'

'No. Mean, my da died when I was wee, so it was me and my maw just. These other guys she was with sometimes, but mostly it was just us.'

They walk on in quiet for a while. If the two of them are in fact ages, then it's actually possible they would have been there at the same time. He is tempted asking him what years he used to go, but he stops himself. Something about Beans, this sense that he doesn't want pinning down and it's the better no to push him on things. Who's he to talk but? He who bloody cloys up at the barest mention of anything that might make him have to remember.

Beans is still on at it as they get back into the park. Ye mind the fiddle player on the Wemyss Bay ferry? Ye go the Punch and Judies? The pleasure boats? The tackle shop and dangle your line through the cracks in the pier? Mick is listening, but he's trying as well to figure out how they are going to make up the price of a bottle and get through the rest of the day.

'Once or twice we stayed in a caravan but most times my maw would be thumbing it through the small ads for one of they rooms that families rented out for the holidays. And see my da, he was a bevvy-merchant, right, and he was always away to the whisky booths or else he was there drinking in the room. But this landlady I mind we had, she knew what like the score was, and I don't know if it was cause it was her weans' room normally or what it was, but she starts into him this time – "Ye can't bring your drink in here, this is my house, a terrible man ye are" – and all this, and me and my maw and my wee sister are sitting there like three pounds of mince, thinking he's gonnae belt her, a pure certainty that he will. But he doesnae. He gets up just and he lets himself out the door, away to the whisky booth, and the three of us and the landlady staring at each other with nay clue what to do next.'

He is sitting on the bench, laughing, as if it's a happy memory he's just recalled.

'Amazing, eh, you going to Rothesay, no think?'

Without the money for a drink, it leaves a hole in the afternoon, so they decide what they'll do is go up the river and pay the swan a visit.

The gate has a new padlock on it. 'Bastards.' Beans strains over the palings, then is off scooting down the path. The swan is out. Or maybe she's been evicted too. The nest is still there, but the whole area has been cleaned up: the cans and the rest of the rubbish gone, and new wiring over the tunnel entrance. They sit down on the veranda and throw chuckies at the floaters, Beans starting up about the Fair again. It is all there in what he's saying – the Winter Gardens, the beach, Italian ice creams – but for some reason there is something queer about how he's telling it, as if it's no true somehow. Like he's heard all this off somebody else but he thinks it's his own memories. Or he's making it up. Maybe it's just himself but, trying to find holes in it. Maybe he doesn't want to believe it's true.

Later, they have a walk down the water. Beans tries it on, tapping passers-by for a few coins, but without much luck. They don't have any change on them; or they don't speak. Head down. Eyes to the tarmac. No a total disaster though. Eventually they come past a young pair kisscanoodling, who give him a two-pound coin.

The gloaming is come on when they return to the park. They drink the single can that they've each got, and take their positions, Mick on the ground with the blanket, Beans up on the bench. Without much superlager inside to numb him up, it is impossible to get to sleep. The cold nipping, and this unsettling feeling going through him in waves that is related he knows to the bringing up of old memories. He must doze off at some point though, because he is dreaming about a paddleboat and a boy fallen off the side when he is suddenly woken up – noise, heat, and a great blaze of fire above him that he realizes, through the flames, is Beans.

He is stumbling, flapping about, his chest and arms ablaze. Mick blunders to his knees, the fire crackling, a smell of petrol. 'Keith,' he shouts, uselessly, pushing him onto the ground and only then clocking the group of men stood on the play area. Watching; walking over. The guy from earlier, a can in his hand, laughing. Beans is thumping his hands on the grass and Mick tries to roll him, this kind of growling noise coming out of his throat, and his face damp, pieces of skin peeling off his neck. The hat – if it caught fire – and he scrabbles to pull it off him, Beans's eyes pleading, crapping it he's going to die. And Mick is thinking it too but he knows, in that instant, rocking the body on the grass, that his own fear is for himself. The men are stood over them. One of them puts an arm out and lager is pouring down, hissing on the dying flames. He is powerless, he just keeps rocking the great charred mass back and forth, burning his hands, until the fire is almost out, and he tries then to take the jacket off but it is too tight – more laughter – so he tears at it and it comes apart in pieces. One of the men suddenly puts the boot on, kicking Beans in his side. Then another of them catches Mick in the stomach and he is keeling over, bent double on the hot grass, no able to breathe.

They are away, running down the path, jumping the gate. 'Keith. Ye alright, pal?' Stupit question. He's alive but. The lips are quivering in his raw bleeding bawface; wet, red patches on his chin and cheeks. Mick pulls off the shreds of his jacket and his shirt, trying no to look at the body, then he takes off his own coat and rests it on top, lying down beside him, his hands stinging, too done in the now to move or think about getting somewhere safe.

30

Beans is sat up on the bench, quiet. He's got the coat draped over him like a blanket, but underneath it's possible to see what's left of his clothes, stuck to him in black tatterings on his chest and belly, patches of red wincing flesh, skin bubbles.

'Ye're well fired, then.'

No the right thing to say. He isn't amused. Just sat there, staring ahead. He's got his woolly hat back on, turned now a darker shade of red. Below it, one of his bug-ladders is burnt off, a few blackened stems of hair poking out from the blistered skin, and the bottom of his ear is yellow and gluey with pus, like an upturned clam.

'Want something to eat?'

Beans shrugs his shoulders just. Gives a kind of snort. Clear enough what he's meaning: who's going to get it, well? Mick stands up and goes to the bin. It hasn't been emptied yet from yesterday and it's overflowing: a magazine and an empty Lucozade bottle sticking out the top. The best he can find though is a bit of brown banana left in its skin and a few crisps in a bag. He takes them over to lay beside Beans on the bench, but he doesn't even turn his head. All the life is went out of him.

He sits again on the bench, the crisps and banana between them.

'I've seen a guy on fire before,' he says then, just to be saying something. 'A welder. Just pure unfortunate, really, cause he was doing this job that he had his mask on for and as well one of these flame-retardant suits, but see that was the problem. He starts jigging about and nobody knows what he's up to at first, they think he's dicking around, but actually a spark is got inside the suit and nobody can see that his clothes is on fire cause, like I say, the suit's flame-retardant.'

Beans isn't listening. His head is sunk down, looking at the grass. There is a scorched patch in front of where they are sitting.

'Anyway, so by the time his mate's clocked what's going on the poor guy is almost fried, and when he comes back from the hospital he's got third-degree burns and everyone's telling him he should go the courts but he says he's no gonnae because it was his own fault for no doing the neck studs up.'

'This supposed to be cheery?'

Mick turns round, relieved. 'Right, sorry.' He smiles. 'Sorry. See what I mean is it could've been worse.' Beans is looking now at the banana and crisps, not moving. His lips are swollen and bluish. 'Worse,' he says, in a quiet voice.

There is the problem of food and also, now, the problem of where to stay. They don't discuss it but it's clear enough they need to move from the park. As well, Beans is in blatant need of some medical attention. When Mick says they should go the hospital, however, he just gives a wee laugh. It's the only thing he responds to all afternoon. The rest of the time he just sits there in silence, pulling the coat around him and covering his wounds, but Mick can see well enough what like the state he is in: his face and neck hugely swollen by now, and the top of the coat soaked with whatever it is that's running out of his sores.

Later, Mick gets up and tells him he's going off to find some food. He starts down the road, looking in the bins. A few people watching him as he gets grubbing inside them but he's too hungry to care, pulling and digging at all this stuff that the residents have decided isn't fit for them any longer: magazines, a bunch of flowers, newspapers with this picture of a politician type on the front. There is food too, plenty of it. Sandwich cartons, some with just the crust left, but a couple that there's actually an entire half-piece in there. Unfuckingbelievable, really. In another bin he finds a Japanese roll left in one box and two more with these pink pickled frillies on the side. He gets it all into a pair of sandwich cartons and leaves back to the park.

He lays it all out on the bench. Beans nods his head slightly – one eye is half closed, the lid above it pink and inflamed – then he stares off again without touching the food, back into whatever it is he's thinking.

They wait it out the afternoon until the light starts to change and Mick gets them on the move. Beans doesn't argue. He doesn't do anything, just keeps cloyed up, loundering slowly behind as they go down the road. They come again to the doctor's practice. He leads Beans down a path to the back of the building. All the lights are turned off and the car park is empty, so he lays the blanket down under an archway by the back door. He sits Beans up against the wall and sets off for more food.

Strange but it's gave him something of a punt up, what's happened. Fucking terrible, of course, he's a terrible bastard to think it but it's true. He feels more of a purpose about him. It's down to himself the now. Showing Beans that he's no just some leech that can't get by on his own. He can be useful. He is being useful. After a long walk he finds a full bin round by a kebab shop. A few looks but so what? Go fuck yourselves. On the way back, it starts to rain. He gets a hurry on, clutching the warm carton of collected chips and doner meat under his jacket.

Beans has moved. The blanket is laid out still, an empty carrier beside it. The rain tearing out from a gutter, hammering onto the concrete.

He eats half the food. Watches the yellow flowers over in the bed, nodding, drooping. Puddles growing in the car park. Which gives him an idea, and he gets up to go on another bin search, eventually finding an empty Coke bottle. Nobody on the street but. When he returns to the pitch he props the bottle with a stone out in the rain.

With the damp, and no overcoat, he sleeps fitfully the night, waking frequently with the same familiar sense of alarm. The blanket bare next to him. By morning, the rain has stopped, and the bottle is filled up quite a bit, stood there in the half-light of the glistening car park. Beans is gone still. He stays there, awake, the sun coming up and the sound of traffic increasing on the road, until eventually there's no choice but to move on before anyone arrives.

He sits on top of a wall across the road, watching the entrance to the car park. The cleaner arrives. He watches the dim shadow of him through a window, slowing passing the mop. Doctors. Patients. A woman with a screaming snapper in a pram, halting and shouting at it to get shut up.

There is curtain-twitching going on behind him. He can see the movement in the corner of his eye when he turns his head to look down the road. Next thing the meat wagon will be blaring up the way, nay doubt. Well, get to fuck, then, he isn't doing anything; he's just sat there. But then what happens, it's no the polis, it's the man of the house opening the door and coming out. 'Excuse me.' The wife in the doorway behind, in her dressing gown. He's got a T-shirt on – DUBLIN MARATHON FINISHER – and he means business: it's his wall, get the fuck off it. 'Excuse me, can I help you?' Mick starts to laugh. The residents don't know what to make of that though, they're exchanging glances, wondering what's their next move. Aw, sod off, and he hops down from the wall, gets walking away down the pavement. That's him, then. No use waiting there any longer, so he decides to go to the river and check the veranda.

No sign of him. A hundred places he could be.

He spends the night at the doctor's. Cold, shaking. Panic sticking the boot on at every turn and keeping him from sleep.

The familiar places: the river, the park – he even starts toward the day centre one morning, but then as he's on the approach he turns about. An ache is growing inside him, taking over the whole of his body. Hunger, for one thing. Something else but. Too big. It's too big. A sense that is inseparable as well from needing a drink – a pure desperate fucking need for one. So he starts going up the coach station again. It takes him a long while to walk there, using the wee bus stop maps and getting lost all the time but so what? Kills the time. Can ye spare any change, madam? Spare any change, sir? They can't. Or some of them can, but most of them give him turned shoulders and the silent treatment. He doesn't care. He needs a drink, simple as that, and everything else – it's all a great blank space above the clouds, himself lying there on top with the hands behind the head and the blanket underneath him, slipping and floating across like he's on a magic carpet. Any change, sir? Ye don't? Nay danger, don't worry, don't worry. An auld hen, her hands tucked together, that way auld ladies do, fingering in her bag. God bless ye, madam. A man gives him his apple and he goes over to Newcastle to eat it, hid inamongst the legs and dragged suitcases as the driver appears with his cup of coffee, climbing onto the coach and getting the doors open. A few moments of noise and bustle. Singsong voices. A wee man walking past, joking with his mate. Somebody he minds him of. Who? Sure there's somebody, and then he does mind – Ken – and he smiles at the memory. A great guy. About four foot two in his work boots, and a smile like a shopping trolley pulled out the river. One of the platers at Swan Hunter. This great singing voice he had on him, always belting out something or other – 'You ain't seen nothing like the Mighty Quinn' – that was one he was always giving it, because Newcastle had this striker at the time that was banging in thirty goals a season.

The bay is thinning out now, a line of people forming outside on the coach park.

The other thing about Ken, most people never guessed until it was too late, he was a serious hardman. He'd bring in his own pieces every day, which the wife had made for him in these neat paper bags. Ham and pease pudding. Every day. He was aye particular about it. What sandwiches you brought today, Ken? And it was funny because he never knew you were kidding, he was that proud of the wife's pieces. So one day this plater's helper called Tommy Lambton thinks it'll be a great joke to take the pieces from under his work bench and hide them while he isn't looking. Come lunch break and Ken's raging. Which of you's took em, then? And suddenly he's got the whole plating squad lined up, blank-faced, because in fact nobody does know where they are, until eventually young Tommy can't hold it in any more and he starts knotting himself – they're here, Ken, and he hands the sandwiches back, fair squashed and grubby by now. That's the end of it, as far as anybody thinks. But later the lunch break Tommy is in the canteen sat down eating, yapping about the great trick he's pulled, when in steps Ken, who comes toward the table and, calm as a waiter, picks up Tommy's plate and walks off with it. Then they're all following him through the yard like he's the Pied Piper, Tommy included, quiet as a mouse now and with this black-affronted look on him, as Ken goes up to the launching berth and tips the food into the water. Then he hands the empty plate back to Tommy and leaves, all the rest of them watching this pie case slowly floating down the Tyne. One guy joking that it just goes to show how much filling they put in those bloody pies.

He laughs at the memory of it. A woman reading her magazine

in the next bay, frowning at him. Chichester, she's going to. Course she fucking is. He gets up and leaves her to it; resumes with his collecting.

There is enough for a couple of cans and a sausage roll. He goes up the river, the old spot, looking out over the power station and the tollie tug. He doesn't stay long though. Even with the drink, he can't get relaxed. Not on his own. The panicky feeling is there, the heart going, some part of him always on the alert now it's only him to keep lookout, and as well nothing to distract him, nobody in his ear giving it the problem with bird-murdering farmers and all the rest.

The park is empty. No weans, or mothers, nothing. It's a pretty dreich day but. The patch of charred grass is still there, less black than it was, but just as dead. He moves on. Down the road he nicks into a pub to go for a pish, but it's dead inside and the landlord cops onto him before he can get in the toilets. Another pub opposite but, and he slips in unnoticed. He washes his face, and nabs a toilet roll from one of the cubicles.

Further on there is a subway station, and he sits down by the cash machines without too much of a thought but that he needs to sit down, so he may as well do it here and tap some money into the bargain. Pure murder on the arse after a while though, even with the blanket and his carrier of clothes underneath him. Thickets of legs, coming in waves, up the stair from the subway. He doesn't look at them. No up at their faces. He keeps his eyes on their ankles and their shoes instead. Without the body and the face on top, the feet take on a life of their own, like it's the feet themselves that are wanting to get a hurry on, them that are annoyed at having to swerve around him. That's fine but. Fine. Feet, he can deal with.

The first afternoon, he makes 87p. The next day, the weather is better and he gets there earlier. Somebody drops him a baseball cap, which he puts on to shield his face from the sun. Another gives him a cup of tea, and when he's finished it he leaves the empty cup on the ground next to him. His earnings almost double. Chink. In it goes. Like pressing a button. He spends his nights in the usual spot behind the doctor's, awake already and away early the morning. Sandwich, superlager; easy enough, the routine, and it gathers around him like a fog, guiding him and protecting him. Inside it but, thoughts and memories appear suddenly like figures out of the mist – he tries to lose them, give them the body swerve; always the same race between the reminders and the drink.

He's slept right through and they are come to move him, the light up and a crowd of blue jackets moving through the car park, one of them picking up an empty bottle of superlager, Beans not there, these rub-ye-ups grabbing at his legs – come on, come on – a man craning down toward him, his face tight with disgust.

The buses. A much better idea. Good and bad points but, obviously. Good and bad. There is a stretch of road with four or five bars knuckled together, and he learns after a couple of tries elsewhere that this is the best place to get on, wait while they're closing and the stops are birling with drunkens trying to cram and heave through the doors. Once on, up the stair and to the front is the best spot, a bit of extra space for the legs and the pilot's view out the window. The smell of chips and vinegar. Kebabs. Listening to the songmakers away at the back. It's only when the front's been took and he has to sit further down that people start putting the mix in. A lassie on her mobile phone sat next to him with her face turned to the window, speaking in a quiet voice and no realizing or caring that he can hear what she's saying. Another time, he falls asleep right in the thick of all these posh, clammering English boys, and wakes up to them laughing, the aisle full of legs and the one sat next to him wearing his baseball cap. The rest of them in knots about it. He sees Mick awake and turns toward him, grinning, takes the cap off slowly and puts it back on Mick's head. He closes his eyes. Too tired to do anything. 'Fuck off.' But that just sets them going again.

When the bus gets further out of the city and it starts to empty, is when he can sleep. Sometimes he'll have a carrier with some cans and he'll drink them up against the seat in front until he's knocked himself out and he sits slumped against the window, eventually the lights shuddering and turning off. Then shuddering on again. The bus starting to move, back toward the city; tired-looking African and East Europe types getting on, staring silently ahead, keeping to themselves.

No uncommon that a fight will break out. He tries to keep out the way, but one night there is one that kicks off across the aisle from him, a proper frontpager. Two pale lads laughing and shouting, going at the staring matches with anybody that looks over. One of them lights up a fag, the smell of it drifting through the bus. Right in front of them, this great belly man in a rock music T-shirt and a kind of perm haircut tumbling over the back of his seat, and the two lads start pishing about, kidding on they're going to set the perm alight. Then the smoker starts blowing smoke past his ear, leaning in so close it looks like he's about to kiss him on the neck. The big guy is getting irritated, tapping the foot and muttering away in a language that's no English. The whole thing kicks off the instant one of them touches the back of his head, and he jumps up and turns around, suddenly clambering onto the seat and standing on it. The two lads totally blindsided, sat staring up at him.

'You wanna see my poothy?'

Giggling from somewhere up the front of the bus.

'You wanna see my poothy, hey?'

The lads don't know what to do; they're sat watching, rigid and seething, and then suddenly the big guy starts into a lap dance, practically in the one boy's face. 'You wanna see my poothy?' And it's more than the boy can take, leaping up and getting the hands around his neck, pushing him back over the next seat and exposing the giant belly from under the T-shirt. Men jumping in now, a young guy in front of Mick standing up but his girlfriend pulling at his arm trying to stop him. There's four or five of them holding the lad back, his mate one of them, but the boy's beeling still, desperate to get at the lapdancer, who is walking away down the aisle by now. The veins standing out on his forehead and the whole face looking like it's going to explode from the skin – eyeballs, teeth, the lot. And then it does. A couple of girls in front screaming as his nose busts, wee red missiles flying everywhere.

31

'Tell you what, I'll give you a call after I speak to Kenny . . . He's coming on straight from college, I think . . . He won't have, but I'll ask him. Okay, got to go.'

The boy puts his phone into his jeans pocket and waits. The woman in front of him is literally taking forever. He glares at her back. When finally she does take her card out he steps forward, but she's not moving, she is staying by the machine, and now she is actually putting the card back in. Unbelievable.

When the woman at last shuffles off and it is his turn, he hesitates a second by the machine, unsure how much money to get – whether or not the plan is to get some food before they go in. He takes out thirty, turning away from the tramp on the pavement, and slips it into his wallet before he moves into the crowd of people streaming toward the tube station.

It is easier in the daytime. Mostly he can sit there for hours and hours without thinking about anything, watching the feet just and then sometimes, chink, and he'll look up at them walking away, a back of the legs and a backside, disappearing down into the subway. He never drinks in front of them. Common sense, that's all. He saves the bevvying for the end of the day when he leaves, and he always spends up whatever he's got, meaning the good days usually are followed by bad ones. Sat there the morning, turning green on the pavement. The sweats. The shudders. Shivering against the wall trying no to move his eyes, and the heart torn and flapping from the paranoia that is rising up inside him that any moment one of these pairs of feet coming out the subway are going to belong to somebody he knows. A total conviction building that Robbie is on the approach. He tries to fight against it but it's hopeless, hopeless, he hasn't the strength, he just wants to sleep, to sleep, to forget and let the brain go numb but he's too fucking sober and his breath is dying each time Robbie's haircut emerges up the stairs. He closes his eyes but it's impossible to stop the sense of him coming toward where he's sat; and then he has to look up – but he's gone, lost into the crowd.

The middle of nowhere. A bus depot. Quiet streets and closed shops. A car showroom; a cemetery; a golf driving range that it is easy enough getting round the back of and into one of the alcoves. It's actually quite comfy there on the spongy green felt with the wooden roof over his head, looking out over the field with its distance markers and a tractor perched at the side.

Screw the buses. There is an office block close to the subway, a big concrete one with dark, morning make-up streaks down the side of it. It is set back from the road, and there's a large, covered doorway at the top of some steps, in front of a revolving door. The lights kept on the night, so it's no the darkest, but see maybe that's in fact a good thing, because even if he is visible, so as well is any other cunt that wants to come along and get acquainted. He huddles in against the doors and gets drinking. Big, frequent gulps, anxious to be bevvied quickly, obliterate the memory. Through in the reception there is a grand flower display, an empty desk, and on the wall beside it a black-and-white TV screen flicking between images of the building: vacant corridors; an office floor; the bare insides of a lift. Nobody anywhere. It looks like the nuclear bomb has gone off. Fucking Trident, man, crank up the engines, float her up the Clyde. But then, the queerie shot of himself, bundled in the doorway. The only survivor. He gives a wave and sees his arm moving. Just him, then. The rest of the world is finally went away. Cheers. The head swimming now. Cheers to that, well.

The cleaners come when the clock in the reception is showing just the back of six, and he has to get up and move on. They are alright about it, being fair, but it's obvious that staying put isn't an option. It is cold, that time the morning, and he is stiff and sore from the ground and the drink, so he walks around for a couple of hours to get the blood going before making his way to the subway. A giant bruise is looming all down his side. He hitches up his shirt and jacket and he can see that the whole area is raw – no a great purple job, but kind of flamed and scarlet, like a rash. Maybe it is a rash, actually. Either way but. He isn't keen on investigating.

The streetlights are still on, and the pavements almost deserted. A few unchancy types. A damp, pink jogger labouring by. He comes after a while to a high street, and there is more action: shutters ratcheting up; a delivery van reversing; the soaked front patch outside a newsagent's. He is a ghost. Nobody seeing him. He walks on down the pavement. An Asian man in a butcher's coat is opening out a board by his shop window: *Star Buy – medium fresh chicken. £2.50 kg.* He starts chuckling. Medium fresh chicken. Good luck with that one, pal. And then he sees that the guy is an exact Asian John Virgo, serious, he is, and that just makes him laugh the more. The delivery van is parked outside. The back doors are open, and two more Asian men are handling what looks like a skinned sheep, hung over the one guy's shoulder as he goes into the butcher's, dark stains all down his coat. The limbs on the animal joggling lifelessly, like a tired wean over a da's shoulders. As Mick walks on past the van, he sees the second guy stood inside it, twisting another carcass out of a pile and lobbing it toward the back doors, where it falls on the wooden boards with a wet thump.

Up the way, a charity shop is open already. A business type stood outside, fingering through a row of books on a trolley. He steps up and stands in beside him, pulling a book off the trolley and starting to give a flick through the pages. A sideways glance from your man, but so what, serious? He slots the book back in and gets reading the spines, and halfway along the row his gaze is checked.

He reaches to take the book but his hand is shaking. A noise coming up his throat but he is only dimly aware of it, the man looking at him, walking away. *Remember,* by Barbara Taylor Bradford – 'An Unforgettable Tale of Passion and Suspense'. He looks up. Through the window, a woman is bent over, rummling inside a plastic bag, and he slips the book under his jacket and moves away.

Somebody brushes against his arm and his body stiffens, the whole of him suddenly turned cold. He doesn't know where he is but there are crowds pouring down the street and he is searching through them, stupit, stupit, but he can't stop himself, desperately trying to mind her face, but he can't.

32

There is somebody coming toward him. A man. He's on the approach from the road, coming up the steps, a carrier in his hand, and Mick is started to tighten, the bevvy no taken hold yet and this cunt in front of him all too fucking real.

'Would you like a sandwich?'

He is holding one out toward him, like a bone.

'It's fine, take it. There were some left we didn't sell.'

He looks at the sandwich in the guy's hand, tightly wrapped in cling film.

'What type is it?'

He brings it to his face, inspecting the filling.

'Not sure. Prawn, I think.' He holds it out again.

'Ye have any beef?'

The man gives a wee laugh and pauses, then gets rustling about in the bag.

'No. He brings out another. 'Tuna?'

Mick shakes his head. 'I'm alright.'

He is staring at him. 'You don't want any of these sandwiches?'

'No.'

A wee lift of the eyebrows.

'Okay, then. Fair enough.' And away he goes. The Master of Sandwiches. Fuck you, pal. Who's he getting annoyed a person doesn't want to take his leftovers? He doesn't like fish sandwiches. That simple. The smell of them. One of the only things he can mind about his da, he used to eat these tins of pilchards, and the stink when they were opened, it was honking.

Sandwiches. Always fucking sandwiches. They never come and offer you a bloody bottle, do they?

*

He is sat on the blanket staring at the book, the sun gone behind the clouds. He takes his cap off and looks out at the pavement. An empty can rattling along the fence with the wind.

'Fuck me. A man of riches.'

He looks up. It is Beans. Stood over him, grinning, peering into the cup. He bends down and sits against the wall next to him. His neck and the side of his face are red and leathery, his ear a great black scab.

'Check you – in the money, eh?' He points at the cup. There is the rumble of a train underneath the ground. He is stretching himself out, sticking his legs onto the pavement. Mick closes his eyes. Tries to make sense of things. It's too much an effort but, and he opens them again, looking across. Beans has got a blue jumper on, a tear down the side of it, his head turned away toward the cash machines; a big peel of skin coming off behind his ear. A moment later and he is lumbering to his feet.

'Come on. Ye hungry?'

Mick doesn't move. The eyes fixed on him from under the dirty red hat.

'No. I'm sticking it out here.'

'Aw, right.' He stays there, dawdling, pedestrians trying to get past. 'I'll see ye, well.'

The rest the afternoon is sunny and he gets quite a few drops. He doesn't feel relieved, or angry, or anything, about Beans. As if he wasn't really there, he imagined him just.

He is real enough though. He appears again as Mick is about to get leaving, a carrier of lagers with him. Mick gets up his things and they are away up the road together to find somewhere to drink it. Simple as that. Back into the routine without so much as a word about all this time that's passed. Easier just carrying along with it. And immediately he is feeling safer. Which is stupit, obviously, seeing as all the unchancy situations he's been in it's because Beans has put him in them. He's got the beers in but. The one thing he can always be relied on for. They sit on a bench in a drab concrete square and get drinking.

'See me, I wouldnae beg. Mean, begging's fine – I've done it myself.' He is scratching at his throat. 'But thing is ye're a sitting

37

He tells Renuka to write back to Missing People. He is safe and well. He will get in touch with them when he is able. Pathetic. It makes it sound like he's been fucking kidnapped.

Beans is back heavy on the drink, and they are returned now to the old routine. Away up the park and into the superlager. A few times Beans puts the mix in with the East Europes by the trees – for some reason he's decided that's where he wants to be sitting, and what right do they lot have taking the best spot? A couple of shouting matches but Mick is able to pull him away and get over the other side of the park before they both get skelped. One night, they have been drinking all afternoon, the both of them totally away for oil, and they don't make it back to the hostel. They find a line of bushes along a path and collapse into it. The night is warm and still, and he lies there awake with the familiar warm weight of Beans pressed up against him. Safe and well. Blootered in a bush next to a madman, his head blaring with drink and sunburn, but he is safe and well, thank Christ for that.

When he is not up the park, he stays in his room with the television on, staring at it, or out the window. Thoughts about the wife, the family, hovering around him the whole time now. He doesn't try to hold them back, there's nay point, and sometimes it builds and builds until he feels like getting up and putting his fist through the window – but instead he just lies there on the bed, staring or greeting. That is another thing he's doing a lot of the now, greeting. It comes on him out of nowhere: sat absently watching a cookery programme and suddenly he's bubbling up and it will go on uncontrollably for a long while, until his face is as hard and sticky as if he's just woke up under a tree. He lets himself do it; he encourages it even, searching for how many ways he's failed her, trying and no being able to get a sense of her, and then blaming himself for that as well.

A chapping at the door. He ignores it. A few minutes later and it's there again. He tries to blank it out, but the heart is going and he knows that much more of this and his nerves will be that ripped he'll have no choice but jumping to his bloody death on the pavement below. He gets up and looks through the peephole. It is Paul. 'You alright in there, mate? Mick? Everything okay, mate?' He stays as still as he can and tries to control his breathing. After a while, Paul goes away. The sound of his door closing.

Renuka has been informed he's stopped going to the art classes and has missed his benefits interviews. She is concerned about him. His eyes and his face and the general honk of him nay doubt pointing to the drink. Is the letter still troubling him? Does he want to think about a different course of action? Aye, I think we should get the whole family down here for a visit, have a tour round the place; then wipe the slate clean, let bygones be bygones.

Paul comes in the kitchen one evening while he is waiting for a plate of food in the microwave.

'How's it going?'

'Okay, thanks.'

'Not seen you at the art class for a while.' He pulls a packet of ready-grated cheese out of the fridge. 'Fancy a knock on the pool table later?'

'Think I'll give it a bye the night, thanks.'

'No worries, no worries. If you do – just give me a knock, right.'

More and more, he is going over the time when she was ill. He tries to mind it, what like it was, what happened, how much of it he was there for. He hadn't finished working until a few months from the end – he couldn't, even after he sold the car, they couldn't afford otherwise – but he can't stop the thought of her alone in the house, in the bed, knowing she was going to die. See if they knew she wasn't going to live, why was he working? Who was he working for? The rent, bills, food, keeping things going, how could any of that have been for her? The smell of the house when he came in off a shift. Going up the stair and seeing her, alone, asleep. Or with Craig. There at the bedside with her. All the wee details, he strains to mind them. Who had called round the house; what had he cooked for her; when did it first come up, the talk of putting in a compensation claim?

As well, an image he keeps recalling. She is picking up the front door mat, taking it outside and shaking it. He recalls it over and over, screwing the eyes trying to make her turn round, see her face, but it is always the same picture: him looking from the doorway, watching her beat the mat on the gate and a cloud of white dust puffing out with each clout. He dreams about this scene and when he is awake he finds himself searching for it, until he doesn't know any more if it is actually a memory, or if he's made it up.

38

His benefits have been cut, and they are threatening to withdraw them on account of the missed interviews. As a result he has no money and he is got behind with his service charge. He keeps to his room. Reads a lot. A new Barbara he's picked up, about this successful businesswoman that owns a string of international inns. She is preparing for her daughter's wedding when she finds out she's suffering from this strange illness that nobody can diagnose, and the only way she can find out what's wrong with her is to go round the world uncovering all these secrets from her past.

All day and all night, even if he's no directly thinking about it, he has an awareness of the family out there, somewhere. Searching for him. Fine well clear enough, the message he's sent out, that he doesn't want to be near them. Pure torture, thinking about it, but that's what he's engaged in – here's my brain, my body, let them fucking stiffen each other. He isn't interested in deadening himself with the drink any more; the torture is more relieving. No that he's gave the drink the go-by but. He still gets to the offie with what little he has on his tail. It's too instinctive not to.

An anxiousness is welling inside him that he cannot leave them hanging like this; himself, hanging. To keep them thinking that he doesn't want to see them. Because he does; he does want to see them. Not all of them, obviously. But the boys – the pull of seeing them, it's undeniable, and it wrests and knots at him because no matter how strong it gets, that pull, it's never as strong as the one that is wanting to keep them away, to keep them from seeing him here.

Up until the letter he had been doing well, at least they seemed to think so, going the classes and up the broo office. He tells Renuka that he's going to start again with the activities, that he's cut out the drink. He goes to the next art class. Everybody says it is good to see him. Maybe they've been talking. Possible they know the score.

Unlikely but, seeing as he hasn't told anybody about the letter, even Beans, who has been going through his own dark patch of late. They have been doing clay objects, bowls, ash trays and that. He makes a small pot, and digs up some soil and a wee flower in the park to put in it; sticks it on the windowsill next to the other one. It dies a couple of weeks later, and he washes out the pot to use as a mug for tea and superlager.

To have something to focus on, something to do, it is good for the nerves. Paul is going to the art classes too and he takes him up on the game of pool. Mick cuffs him. No that Paul seems to mind. He's happy just being up there in the day room, it seems, talking. Amazing, all these things he says he's got up to. One story he tells him. Each fortnight when he gets his giro, he draws a twenty out the cash machine and goes straight up the supermarket. The security guards are always on his tail whenever he's there, so what he does, he tries to look as unchancy as he can, jinking in and out of the aisles, giving these shifty wee glances at the guards – then he grabs a bottle of champagne and something else expensive, a steak, or a pack of smoked salmon, and he slips them under his coat and legs it to the tills. Just as the heavy team are sweating and shouting up the aisle, he sticks them on the belt and pulls out the twenty, all calm and swaggersome, and the meatheads are left standing there just, panting and stupit. He's okay, is Paul. He's been on a script the last six months, he tells him, and he's trying to sort himself out. There is a woman that comes round quite often to visit him: his girlfriend, Monica, who he knows from when he lived up north. She's friendly too. A couple of times she comes in the day room and chats with them while they're playing pool.

Renuka and him talk about whether he feels ready to start with the move-on process. Yes. A pure certainty he is. She explains to him that he needs to get his service charge on track, and then she lays out how it works: that they get given a quota each year to put on the housing register; that it's no a very big quota; that it might take some time. Fine. Whatever it takes. He is compliant.

Posters go up around the hostel for an outing to an open-air theatre production in the park. Beans and Paul are dead set on going, so he puts his name down. A sunny day, when it arrives, and the play

is in fact quite enjoyable. It's about this young Asian girl who is supposed to marry a guy she's never met, but she's fell in love instead
with a white lad that works on the market. Racial differences. Argle-
bargling families. Eventually the pair try to escape and there's a
tragic ending in a cash-and-carry car park. Pretty interesting, parts
of it, although you'd think it's actually the ten of them from the
hostel who are the real show, the way the residents stare at them
from their blankets. Beans, at least, enjoys the attention – laughing
loudly at all the jokes and getting up each while to walk a circle
around the back of the audience, his hands clasped behind him,
smiling and pattering away.

He meets Renuka in the computer room and she shows him how to
go the internet and get looking at properties. Incredible, really, all
that just there at the fingertips. She has to demonstrate a few times,
the same patient way she explains everything else, writing notes on
a piece of paper so he can mind for next time. They put in his bidding number and look together through the vacant flats. A few
decent ones; a few genuine shitholes. She does another session with
him, and he puts a couple of bids in. If he prefers, she can do all this
for him, she says, but he tells her no, he's fine doing it himself. He
wants to do it himself.

There's never many in the computer room. Sometimes one or
two with the giant headphones on, listening to music; and usually
as well the young woman from the art class, sat quietly getting on
with her own things. He doesn't mind coming in here, especially
now the weather is on the turn and the park is cooler and blowier
getting. At least he is out of his room doing something. As well,
there's the anticipation through each week of seeing if your bid's
come in, followed by the inevitable finding out that you've went
down again. One day he is getting up to leave, the same time as the
woman is for the off, and they go out the door together. She slows
down in the corridor, turning to speak to him.

'You're bidding for a council house, aren't you?'

'Aye. Ye doing the same?'

'Yes – four months.'

'Serious? Nothing?'

'Nope. Well, I went to look at one a couple of weeks ago that was just a dump. Everyone ahead of me had obviously turned it down.'

He's no heard her say this much before. Surprising how well spoken she is.

'You on the Clearing House?'

'The – mean, I don't know.'

'Well, maybe better not to be anyway.' They are come to the reception. 'Good luck with it.' She smiles, and goes toward the main entrance.

The longer goes on, the more restless getting he is. Nearly eight months is by now since they notified the charity that he'd fucked off and left them. To get on his feet just, be in a flat. Then he could face them. Face the music. Could he? See that's what he's been telling himself – that's what's been driving him through – but, if it comes to it, is he actually going to be able to look at them and no just wither in a heap at their feet? And as well, who's to say that they do want to see him? Consider that one a moment. There is a hollow feeling he gets when he starts thinking like this. Hard to stave off the drink but he's trying. A loneliness that circles about itself, because then he'll start thinking about Cathy, searching for her, this sense that she is there but out of his grasp; and it leaves him empty, longing.

He speaks to Renuka about the housing situation. The lack of a housing situation. She makes him a tea and puts her doctor's face on. The problem with the letting scheme, she says, is there's crap-all housing stock left in the borough. He can keep on as he is, and points-wise at least he's no badly stacked, but there's no guarantees anything will happen soon. Or, he can try for a private-rented tenancy. More likely he'll get something that way, but more likely as well that it'll be expensive and temporary and the landlord will be a bastard. No quite her words, but he gets the picture.

He asks her to stick him forward for it. At the same time though, he carries on with his internet bidding. The art class girl, Terri, is in the same boat and the pair of them are in there each week, talking about have you seen this house or that house. As well, Beans has got himself involved. No that they're letting him think about getting his own flat – Robin is still doing his box in at how he carries on – but he can't resist getting in the mix, telling Mick which flats he should and shouldn't go for. Amazing, but he's pretty good at working the computers. When he gets bored of looking at the properties, he turns to his own screen and starts pulling up TV shows, news, underwear models. Anybody's guess how he's learnt to do it. In other hostels maybe. Nay point asking him. Sometimes it's easier leaving off the questions and just marvelling at the guy.

His benefits have been mostly restored and he is working at paying his service charge arrears. Still applying for the jobs that he's even less of a sniff of now after the missing period, and starting on something of an economy drive: less bevvying, more of the Barbaras. He is reading one about another female reporter, in Kosovo, whose colleague gets shot and she leaves the war behind to do celebrity photo shoots. This playboy artist she meets and falls for, but everything that's happened in the past continuing to plague her at every turn.

He keeps up with the art classes, and goes a couple of times to a film club that gets run in the day room by a chuckling retired Welshman called Peter. Sometimes as well there'll be an event going on in the hostel. One day, a visit from a member of the English royalty, or the aristocracy, or Christ knows who he is, but Mick comes down to the thing for the same reason everybody else does: because there's a free lunch going. It is an old guy with gold jewellery draped off his blazer, so maybe he's the Lord Provost or something. He shakes the hands, keeps the stiff smile on his face, eats a polite amount of sandwich triangles and mini sausage rolls. The weeks continuing to go by. The outside colder and colder getting and the heating turned up to blasting so that everybody starts wandering about the place in vests and shorts. Occasionally new people being admitted, led numb and shivery through the reception.

His art collection grows to include a fruit bowl with no fruit in it, a painting of a tree and another of Ibrox, a papier-mâché swan and a T-shirt with *Bluenose* stencilled on it. He is passing time, waiting, but when one morning Renuka knocks him up with the news that a private-rented flat is become available, he feels, at the same instant as relief, a sense of foreboding; unsure suddenly if this is what he wants, if it wouldn't in fact be easier staying put where he is.

39

There's no great ceremony about it, thank Christ. No staff lined up to pat him on the back and give him advice. Nobody at the door to collect and drive him away. He packs up his things into a large hold-all he bought in a charity shop and goes down to the reception, where Renuka hands him his new set of keys. She is arranging their meeting for later the week when Beans comes loundering in with a frying pan.

'That you, well?'

'That's me.'

'Good. Great.' He shuffles about a bit, and holds up the fryer. 'Here.'

'Ye got me a frying pan?'

Beans nods.

'Cheers.' He takes it, smiling. The coating is worn off the inside rim and it's quite possible he's lifted it – the skinny neighbour, more than likely – but no the less, no the less, and he stands there looking at Beans as a lump of gratefulness and fear together lands in his stomach.

Beans is grinning. 'Off ye go, well. Flatman.'

The bus goes past another parade of shops and he tries to recognize where he is. To mind which is his stop. No yet. He keeps the eyes trained for the boarded-up pub which is where he has to get out. Nobody is noticing him. Strange, that he's thinking they might, that all of them know the score somehow, when actually they don't even see him. There's the occasional wee keek over from a teenage lad across the aisle, but he realized a while back that he's just looking at the frying pan and papier-mâché swan which are rested on his lap.

He gets off and walks round the corner past the boarded-up pub, acting it that everything is normal and okay as he approaches the building and punches the code in. There is nobody about. He gives the lift a swerve and gets walking up the stair, his feet echoing against the grey painted steps. A couple of floors up, he stops on the stairhead and looks out through a narrow cracked window at the surrounding roads and buildings. Nowhere he recognizes. All of it alien, and he carries on up to his own floor.

It is a room and kitchen type of affair. The main room with a bed against one wall and a small shiny brown settee against the other. A plastic table with two chairs in the middle. When he first came to see it, the landlord said he should feel free to change things around however he wants, and him and Renuka had a wee chuckle about it afterwards. Bed this side, mini settee the other? Or mini settee this side, bed the other – what do you reckon? There is a doorless opening into the kitchen that he goes through now: toaster, microwave and a kettle, which he fills and flicks on. He puts the swan on top of the microwave and the fryer into the empty sink cupboard, then goes to sit down in the other room, listening as the kettle starts to boil.

No tea. Obviously. Or milk. Crap. He goes for a lie down on the bed instead. Closes the eyes, a heavy tiredness now come over him. A no unfamiliar situation. Careful. Just fucking be careful, my man.

He goes out later and finds a chip shop along the main road. Brings back a fish supper. Pretty decent, it turns out.

After sitting the mini television onto the table and fiddling about with it for a bit, he manages to get it up and running, and settles in to watch it. He should have minded to get napkins from the chip shop, because he's put grease marks over the settee, and he makes a note to wipe them off later. Nothing on the tellybox. Crap just. He gets up and goes to the window, looks out again at the city. It is still light outside, and he notices there's no blind. Another thing that will need sorting. Tomorrow, he can make a list or something. In that moment, the great grey expanse of the city stretching out in front of him, it feels all of it too much, and he leans forward to rest his head against the glass. He imagines Robbie and Craig stood there in the bare room, scrutinizing it. All of it, too much.

Ye battle on but. Ye battle on.

He keeps in and about the flat over the next couple of days. Staying busy. Going the messages for bread, milk, ham, beans, washing powder, loo roll. Normal things; normal people things. Then as well the wee chores: washing the clothes, getting them hung on the radiator and the back of the settee, cooking, washing up, pinning the pillowcase over the window. The evenings, he watches the television, eats, drinks a few cans.

On the third day, Beans comes round, the loudness of the entry buzzer surprising him as he's brushing his teeth, causing him to jab himself in the gums. He's at the bottom, the voice comes through the speaker, he needs pressing in. A surprise as well, Mick considers as he waits for him to come up the building, that he has minded the number.

He comes in and looks the place over from the doorway.

'How much is it, this?'

'Hundred and fifty.'

'Fucksake. Terrible.'

He goes up to the window and fingers with the pillowcase a moment, nods his head, then turns about. 'I'd go a cuppa.'

That day, and the next, they go up and down the high street spending his resettlement grant on bits and pieces for the flat. A broom, radio, hammer, nails, wire wool, a blind, bleach. He isn't too sure about the five packs of wire wool, but Beans is adamant it's an essential – keeps the mice out – so he gives in and buys it. He's keeping interested in all this, Beans, longer than he does most things. Possible that he is wanting to prove himself, let Robin see that he's no just some useless troublemaker. Mick is in the main room, investigating for gaps in the skirting boards, when there is the sound of something heavy scraping through in the kitchen. A moment later and Beans steps out, hands on hips.

'Place needs a paint, no think?'

The painting project begins the next day. Probably it isn't allowed in his contract, but so what, screw the landlord, no like he's going to do it himself, is it? Straight away, the place starts looking brighter. The radio on and a cold draught coming through the window, he starts in the main room while Beans gets stuck into the kitchen, his eyes red and squinting with concentration, specks of paint all over his hat and onto the kitchen counter. Mick grins, finishing round the window frame, at the idea of Beans as a neighbour. Knocking him up because he's run out of loo roll, giving it his wild stories, ear-biting him down the pub. No the worst thought, being honest.

It is Beans anyway that gets him acquainted with one of his own neighbours. They are coming out the lift on their way back into the flat, and there is a woman on the stairhead with a baby in a pram and a dog tied to one of the handles. Beans goes straight up to the dog.

'How's it going, big man, eh? How's it going?' He is bent down, patting the dog on the neck. 'He a Staff?'

'Yeh.' She snatches a look into the waiting lift.

Beans is pulling the dog's cheeks back roughly, no that it seems to mind.

'I had a Staff myself, a long while, I had him. He was a great dog. Walter. Like a fucking radiator, man – oh, pardon me.' He looks into the pram. 'True but. See that's how I called him Walter. Walter water bottle.'

She gives a smile, and presses the button as the lift doors close. Beans is moved onto the baby now though, waving at him with the big cabbage hands. 'Gonnae give me a smile, pal? Gonnae, eh?' It isn't looking likely. The baby is transfixed staring at the big red beardie face, trying to work him out, wondering if something frightening has happened to Santa Claus. The doors open again and she gets moving the pram inside.

'Nice to meet you,' Mick says, and she smiles briefly before the doors slide closed.

Awake, asleep, the awareness of Robbie and Craig presses on him all the time. What he would say to them. How their faces would look if they knew where he's been, where he is the now, that he is on benefits. One moment he is saying to himself: fuck it, I'm fixing this out, but then the next moment the whole weight of everything will be holding him powerless on the bed. Even if he was being offered jobs – and each week he goes up the jobcentre it is look-ing the more likely that it's never going to happen – how would he earn enough to pay the rent even? He wouldn't. And that's for a craphole like this. It would take years saving up for somewhere bet-ter. Just thinking about it makes him feel tired as hell, but he makes a deal with himself only to think about it when he's outside, on the move, and no when he's alone in the flat. Plus as well there's only one radiator in the place and it's pure nipping. So, when Beans isn't about, he spends whole afternoons taking these long walks, getting familiar with the local streets and grassy areas, turning it all over in his head.

How can you attack things full pelt when it's enough already just getting through the day-by-days? The way things have been, even the most wee things feel like an achievement, like he's winning. Shaving. Going the messages. Putting a blind up. They're effort enough as it is that the idea of getting those done and then saying – right, well, that's they sorted, now let's crack on for that warehouse job I've been passed over for five times already – it saps all the energy from him.

It's one of the things Renuka talks to him about when he sees her next. He takes a bus to meet her in a cafe for a chat about how he's getting on. She tells him he is at a contemplative stage of his Cycle of Change. A good thing, apparently. Important that he acts on it. Crucial. The next stage looming all the time over him. Does he feel ready? Almost, he tells her, his stomach dropping through his arse onto the bits of lasagne on the floor by his feet. Almost.

It is afternoon and him and Beans are sat in the flat watching television. Beans hasn't spoke in a while, and he is staring now at the adverts, scratching the backs of his hands, his eyes bloodshot, unreadable.

'Ye crabbit, eh?'

Beans ignores him.

'Hey, you,' Mick grins, digging him in the leg. 'Ye crabbit or something?'

He stands up suddenly. 'This is keech, let's go the pub, eh?'

'Sure. Okay.'

The nearest pub is a walk. Beans seems to know well enough where he's headed, and they walk on past the high street, down a couple of quiet residentials.

'I'm on the bell,' Beans says when they arrive, going up to the bar while Mick gets sat at a corner table. The place is quiet. A couple of men playing pool in a small room on the far side, and four regulars on barstools who eye Beans silently as he counts the smash in his hands and asks the barman what the pool table takes.

Mick watches as he goes and puts his coin on the table, the pool players exchanging glances as he does it.

They drink quietly for a bit, Mick staring at the slumped backs of the regulars and the tattered silver Christmas decorations drooping off the gantry. After a bit, he turns toward Beans.

'Know that dog ye were talking about – Walter – when was it ye had him?'

'Jesus, cannae mind.'

Mick takes a drink.

'What was it recent, like?'

'Eh?'

'The dog, was it a long while ago or was it recent?'

'Christ, a long while.' He stretches his neck round to look behind him. 'Fucksake, they no done yet?'

One of the pool players is walking back to the room with a couple of pints.

'What happened to him?'

'Copped his whack, didn't he.'

'Sorry, I didnae mean –'

'Fine. Fine. He was old, he'd done his stretch. I was in this place anyway, I had to give him up, they wouldnae allow dogs.' He turns round again. 'See that? Fucking kidding me?' He pushes his chair back and gets marching toward the pool room, where the two men are racking up for a new game. Mick sits watching, as if through a haze, a dream, the two men standing close together with their pool cues propped on the floor, Beans shouting, he can't make out what over the Christmas pop music. This song, he minds the video, the English comedian and the blonde lassie, what was her name? A line of angled heads at the bar, and Beans bent over the pool table, scattering the balls. Kim Wilde. That's her. Whatever happened to Kim Wilde? Beans away now out the pub doors. The barstool men slowly turning to look at him instead . . . *the Christmas tree, have a happy holiday. Everyone dancing merrily* . . . no these fuckers, serious, look at them. Jesus. He stands up. Gets gone.

Beans is already off down the pavement.

'Hey, wait up. Wait up a moment.'

But he's away. On the march. A cloud of breath above his head. Mick hurries behind, calling out, all the way to the high street. A bus pulling up – Beans makes a run toward it and hops on.

For the next couple of weeks Beans is even more unpredictable with his visits. He comes round twice, briefly, without any announcement, but then over Christmas he is there almost every day. They buy a chicken. Sprouts, tatties, superlager. They fix up a proper feast for Christmas day and fall asleep blootered in front of the television.

He makes Renuka a tea while she sits at the table and looks about the room.

'It looks good in here,' she says when he comes through with the mugs.

'Better, eh? Keith has been helping me get the place fixed out.'

'Good. Actually, that's something I was hoping to ask you about. Keith's key worker wanted to know if he's been round at all. His depression has been quite bad of late, and he's been absent from the hostel a few times. How has he seemed to you?'

'Fine, fine. Normal. He's been a great help, being honest.' He decides no to tell her about the business in the pub.

'Okay, good, I'll let Robin know.' She clasps her hands around her mug. 'So, you said last time that you'd been thinking about us being in touch with Missing People. Have you given any more thought to it?'

He takes a drink of tea and rests the mug on the table.

'Ye might say that, aye.'

40

He is there early, even with the traffic. Time enough for a wee set-
tler before he arrives. It is a big place, pretty empty the now in the
quiet after lunchtime. One of these bright-lit chain affairs, low leather settees around low tables. He gets sat on one of the few normal
table and chairs, near the middle of the room, facing the entrance.
A couple of business types in suits are stood at the bar, drinking
lagers and talking loudly. Mick takes a sip of his half. His giro isn't
due until tomorrow, and he's spent almost the last of his money on
new shoes and trousers. He didn't consider it. The thought then of
Robbie having to buy the drinks. Alarm starting to race through
him again and it's a few minutes before he can get it under control.

He continues to drink slowly. A pure battle no to neck the thing
but he manages to keep nursing it, while the businessmen move
onto the spirits and the bar staff have a short argument what music
to put on, and so he isn't anywhere near as well on as he'd want to
be when, early himself, Robbie walks in.

He hasn't seen him. He's gone straight to the bar, standing in
next to the businessmen and saying something to the barmaid. Mick
stays sat. He looks the other way, toward a television screen with no
sound because all you can hear is the music that is playing over the
speakers. He cannot move; his whole body is turned to mince. On
the screen there is a wee video of footballers on a training field and
the rolling news underneath – the big story from the English League
One is that the Carlisle United manager is for the chop and another
guy is lined up already for the hot seat. He turns around. Robbie is
coming toward him. A pint in his hand, approaching the table.

'Robbie.' He tries to get standing up but he is rooted.

Robbie stands on the other side of the table, looking at him. His
face – he sits down and Mick cannot look at it so he fixes his gaze on
his hands instead, resting flat on the table. How steady they are, his
son's hands.

'How are ye, Rob?'

He knots his own hands together around his pint, and they look like an ale jug, one of they old-fashioned type of ale jugs. A stupit thought to have the now. Stupit. Will he no speak? Is he going to sit there without speaking for the whole duration, however long that will be, the duration, perhaps a fucking lifetime? Mick glances up at him. He is greeting. No bucketfuls, but his face is tightened and the eyes are welled up, and Mick has to look away – will Rafael Nadal overcome his knee injury in time for the Australian Open? At the moment, his chances aren't looking too rosy.

'I don't know what to say to you.'

'Ye don't have to say anything, son.'

The two businessmen are away, one of them laughing and putting the arm around the other's shoulders a moment, then withdrawing it, clapping the hands together. Off blotted back to the office for an afternoon's work. He looks at Robbie, who is watching them leave.

'I'm sorry, Rob.'

There is silence as they take a moment to consider each from their own side of the table how pathetic it sounds.

Robbie turns back toward him.

'What, were you homeless, Da?'

'If that's the word.'

'What else is the word?'

'No, well, it's that one, aye.'

'Mean, you were on the street?'

'Some of the time.'

'Jesus.' He is staring now at the table. 'Didn't you think I would've helped you?'

'I know ye would, son. I know.'

Robbie is screwing his eyes, scowling. 'We didn't know if you were alive. Most of them thought you were dead.'

He hasn't drunk any of his pint.

'I sent a letter.'

'Oh, yeh, your letter. Suddenly I get this letter and me and Alan are come to stay in fucking Heathrow for a month but nobody there knows where you are either, only that you were calling yourself Mick Provan and you got the sack.'

The barmaid is coming toward them. She is carrying a large black drinks tray which she sets down on the edge of their table, and picks up Mick's empty glass to put on it. She hovers by them for an instant, looking like she's about to say something, until she seems to clock that the atmosphere's no the best and she walks away.

'Alan was with you, then?'

Robbie shakes his head slowly. 'Fuck off, Da. He's been bloody great. Do you know it's him that was paying the rent arrears after you abandoned the house?'

He closes his eyes, or the elastic has went. His insides are turned to liquid, the bones alone holding himself on the chair, somehow. How is that? How are they holding him on the chair still? He was fixing things out. He was out the hostel and into a flat and he was fixing things out. He opens his eyes; sits upright in the seat. The thought comes to him suddenly that he is glad he hasn't shat himself.

He tries to say something but no words come.

'Do you understand what I'm saying? Craig's there telling him to –'

'Robbie,' he interrupts him, 'look, I'm sorry but, mean I don't think I can hear all this the now. I'm sorry.'

'What? What is it not a good time or something?' Robbie stands up. 'You're right.' His voice is shaking. 'You're right.'

He steps out from the table and tucks his chair back under. Then he turns, and starts to walk away.

He stays there, sitting. The bar is empty. After a few minutes the music is turned up loud, no paying customers left for the bar staff to worry about, only one old guy on his own sat staring at the sports news.

41

The rest of the afternoon is a wipeout. The door locked; television on. Renuka and Beans no calling round, or if they do he doesn't notice.

He is in and out of sleep the night, the television on in the background, an educational programme he tries to get listening to, occupy the mind – how does the criminal justice system work? – it's boring enough but it doesn't knock him out, and he lies there gazing at the spasm of blue light on the ceiling.

The next morning he is stood in the kitchen waiting for the toaster to finish when the entry buzzer goes. It is Renuka.

She comes in and sits with him at the table.

'I spoke to Robbie yesterday evening. I gather things were difficult.'

'They were.'

'It isn't going to be easy, obviously, as we said before.'

He nods.

'He's quite keen though, your son, to keep trying.'

'Ye think?'

'Well, yes – he's sat in a cafe down the road waiting for me to call him. He wanted to come straight here, but I told him I needed to speak to you first.'

She is smiling but he turns his face away from her. Out the window, it is started snowing.

'What did he say?'

'He just said that you both need to keep trying.'

He looks round at the tiny room: the unmade bed and the child-like paintings on the wall above it.

'I don't know I'm ready, Renuka.'

She is nodding. 'I know. The thing is though, if you leave it like this, things will only be more difficult the next time.'

She is right. They will. Plus as well the boy lives on the other side the world, so nay doubt he'll need to be going back anytime soon; and he is reminded again with a crawing of the stomach that he has come away from his family for this, for ten minutes in a chain bar and the da to tell him he's no wanting to see him still.

'The stupit thing is, I was that bloody terrified going there, I just needed to see him the more.'

She is nodding again. Patient as ever. Plotting where all this puts him on his Cycle of Change; or thinking he's a bastard just, who knows?

He comes in the flat with Renuka and stands in the doorway looking at him.

'Robbie. Come in. Want a cup of tea? Renuka?'

Robbie and Renuka wipe the slush off their feet and go in the main room while he takes the kettle over to the sink to fill it up. He can hear him treading through in the other room, inspecting, judging. Renuka telling him that it's his father that's fixed the place up, with the blinds, the paint job, and Robbie keeping quiet; whatever he's doing in there he's no saying anything about it.

He moves the television onto the floor and they sit down all three of them around the table. Get drinking their teas.

'So,' says Renuka, 'I can be here, or not be here – just tell me which you'd prefer.'

'No,' Robbie says, 'stay. It's fine. Yes?'

He nods.

'Look, Da, yesterday – I didn't mean to be difficult. Just there's things I don't understand.'

'Aye, course.'

'I don't know where to start.'

'No, me neither.'

Robbie is looking at the art work on the wall above the bed.

'You an alcoholic, Da?'

'No.'

Renuka is keeping quiet. It would look better, he realizes, if there weren't the empty cans of superlager on the floor by the bin.

'Just I don't understand how it's happened. If I'd known how things were, I would've stayed. Course I fucking would. Why didn't you say anything? I've felt that fucking guilty.'

'Christ, it's no your fault, Robbie, I didnae know any of this would happen. I should've answered your calls, you're right. Things got on top of me just.'

'Know you've lost the tenancy now? Alan couldn't keep paying it forever.'

He is glaring at him. Challenging him. Mick keeks down at his tea. The mug is chipped already. Pound-shop tollie, what do ye expect?

'I'm no going back, son, if that's what ye mean.'

A long period of silence. Much tea drinking. Renuka glancing from one to the other of them, weighing up when is the right time to step in.

'That's another thing I don't understand,' Robbie says finally.

He waits for him to go on, but he is gone quiet, looking at the table.

'What's that? What ye no understand?'

'That's where she is.'

He looks up, but the face isn't angry, he just looks horrendously fucking sad, which of course sticks the boot on a hundred times worse; and, together with it, he is seized with a feeling of desperate closeness to the boy, of wanting to be close to him.

'That's how I couldnae be there, Robbie.'

There is another stretch of quiet, broken again by Robbie. 'See, even if I can get understanding it, I can tell you for sure, Craig won't.'

Renuka is giving him a pitying look and it seems at that moment like she's about to put her hand on his. He withdraws it, gets it under the table.

'He knows he didn't act right, Da. Neither of you did. When I was staying with him, he said that. But then when you didn't come back, it – he – it was too much for him, I think.'

'Yous two come to blows?'

Robbie gives a wee smile. 'You might say that.'

There is obviously more but Robbie has cloyed up, gazing out the damp window.

'Either of you go another cup of tea?'

Robbie shakes his head. 'No. Thanks. I think we should call it a day for now, okay?'

'Right.'

They all stand up.

'Where ye staying?'

'I'm in a hotel in King's Cross. My flight's booked for next week. I can't leave them any longer.'

Renuka stays in the main room as he steps with Robbie to the door.

'I am glad to see you, you know,' Robbie says, and moves to put his arms about him. Mick comes forward uneasily. It is awkward and odd, being touched, and he stiffens up immediately. He can feel Robbie's chin on his shoulder. After a few seconds, they pull back, and Mick is about to say that he is sorry but he stops himself. He worries how he smells.

'I'll call round again tomorrow, okay? You should get a phone.'

He comes early the next afternoon. They sit on the tiny settee drinking coffee with the television on in the background. There is too much that needs saying to be able to say a lot, so they keep fairly quiet. He does anyway. Robbie is more conversational, if that's the word for it – more an interrogation, which it seems at times he's trying to hold himself back from but he can't; all these questions that he needs answers for. Why didn't he tell anybody he was leaving? Why did he go to London? What happened at the hotel? Why did he write the letter and then not make contact again, even when he was homeless?

If there were straight answers that he could give, then it would be easier. Why *did* he go to London? Why did he do any of it? Christ knows. He needs to be fair but, to be open, so he attempts to tell him at least some of what he's asking, even if he is light on the details.

Later on they try again going for a pint. They give a bye to the bearpit up the way, and walk a while longer in the other direction until they come to a decent-looking place next to a private gardens that is white with a covering of untouched snow. His giro is come and he's able to get the round in. Robbie of course is quick enough asking him how he's living, so he tells him. Whatever he thinks about it, he keeps it to himself. A few others in. A couple of old English boys in ties and blazers. There are things that Robbie wants to tell him: how it's been, all this time without knowing where he was. He was staying with Craig at first, he says, but then it got too much and he rented a temporary place for himself. Eventually he had to go back to Australia. His job. The family. Mick is wanting to ask him about Jenna and Damien, but he can't bring himself to. Before he returned, Robbie tells him, he went down to Newcastle, wondering if maybe that's where he'd went. Trying to dig out anybody he might have worked with; persuading landlords and bookies to let him put up these posters that the charity had printed. The rare time he did find anybody that minded him – how he had to explain the whole story to them about what had happened.

He doesn't want to hear any of this but he knows he has to let him say it. He certainly doesn't ask who it was Robbie found that used to know him. The thought of his mugshot up in a string of pub lobbies, there for every bevvy-merchant to have a gawp at – it's no exactly something he wants to get thinking about.

That evening, when they come back from the pub, he overhears Robbie in the kitchen, talking on his mobile phone. The tap is on while he washes up the plates from their curry carry-out, and Mick is through in the main room with the television on, but he can hear well enough.

'. . . he's got this flat, he's . . . Yeh, I know, I know, but I want to . . . No, it's fine . . . No, he's on benefits.'

The tap is turned off then and Robbie is saying goodbye. He turns the television up louder. Afterward, when Robbie has left, he wonders if he had meant him to hear.

The following morning, Robbie comes round with a new telephone in a cardboard box. As they get opening it, Robbie says that he's spoke to Alan. He wants to come down and see him. Mick keeps quiet and concentrates on the box as he is told this.

'Don't worry. I told him it's too soon. He can wait, but you're going to have to see him sometime, with all he's done.'

'Aye, I know,' he says, even though there's absolutely nay fucking chance in hell he's ever going to let that meeting happen. 'And Craig?'

'I've spoken to him, yes.'

'Doesn't want to see me, eh?'

'He's relieved we've found you, Da.'

'Right.'

'He is.' He puts down a handful of phone entrails. 'He's going to find it difficult that you don't want to be in Glasgow, like I said.'

They get on with taking wires and parts out of the box, arranging them on the floor, and they let the subject go quiet. One thing's for sure: these telephone manufacturers don't like making life simple. Even the phone isn't a phone yet: it's in blocks of plastic that need fitting together. Robbie gets reading through the instructions leaflet, and Mick is started on screwing the handset together, when the buzzer goes. He gets up and answers it. Beans. For a split second he considers telling him it's no a good time, but then the great cargo of guilt that he's carrying everywhere is straight away weighing upon him, and he changes his mind.

This is the first he's seen him in a while. A nervousness builds as he waits for him to come up the lift that he won't be sober, that his clothes will be clatty. He has told Robbie that there is a guy he's known, who helped him when he was on the street, but the most he's said when Robbie's asked what like he is, is that he's from Paisley and he's something of a queer ticket.

Beans is puzzled at first that there is somebody else in the flat.

'This is my son, Robbie.'

'Yer son? Oh, right. How's it going?' He puts a hand out, and Robbie shakes it. 'Keith. Ye come to stay?'

Robbie glances over at Mick, understanding then that Beans obvious isn't up to speed with the situation.

'I'm here visiting for the next couple of days. I'm stopped in a hotel in King's Cross.'

Beans is giving him a quizzical look.

'Where ye from? You an islander?'

Robbie grins. 'Naw. Govan.'

Beans doesn't look convinced. 'That's a strange accent ye've got. I'm no being rude.'

Mick stands in the kitchen doorway, observing the pair of them.

'No, don't worry, my wife tells me the same. I've been living in Australia for ten years, that's how I sound like this.'

Beans laughs. 'I knew it. I knew there was something strange about you. What's all this?' He has spotted the dismembered phone next to its box and is going toward it. 'See me, I'm good with telephones.'

He gets immediately trying to put the thing together. With no little success either. Making Robbie see him over the different coloured wires and screwdriver heads, demonstrating how it's done. Robbie is clear intrigued by the guy. Right from the kick-off there is an easiness between them, which in fact shouldn't be too surprising: he's pretty straight down the line like that, Robbie, takes people as he finds them.

The phone is fixed out in no time. Robbie gives it a call off his mobile phone to check it works. It does. He is connected. He is attainable 24/7 and nay excuses. Robbie notices then that he has a message from Jenna and he goes in the kitchen to make them a cup of tea and get reading it.

'Who's Jenna?' Beans asks when he's gone out the room.

'His wife. They've a wean too, a toddler.'

Beans goes quiet a moment, thinking.

'He come over to see your flat, then?'

'No exactly.' He may as well tell him the score. 'Turns out I've been on this missing persons list for quite a while. They were looking for me.'

Beans is nodding slowly. 'That's good. They've found ye. That's very good.'

The last two days of Robbie's stay pass quickly. The temperature is dipped to freezing but he's bought a new two-bar heater and they keep most of the time to the flat, or the pub, Beans joining them for a pint but keeping on pretty good behaviour. The last afternoon, when Beans goes off, they get wrapped up and go on a long walk, at one point passing the subway station, Mick keeping quiet as they move by. It is good, being around him; he enjoys his company, always has. Strange how you forget. No that it's perfect but.

Obviously. There's moments when he can feel Robbie is gone quiet and he knows that he's thinking about things, withdrawing from him. Fair enough but. Fair enough. Robbie doesn't bring it up but he knows that he is missing the family, and from what he can tell when he's talking to Jenna in the kitchen, she's feeling the same way.

The morning of his flight, they sit in a cafe along the high street eating ham, egg and chips. Robbie says he wants him to come over to Australia for Easter.

'I've talked to Jenna about it. It was her idea, actually.'

Mick looks up at him without speaking. Robbie's got that face on him that says he's ready for a fight if one is needed.

'That's kind of you, son. See but –'

'I'm paying for your flight.'

He shakes his head. 'It'll cost a fortune.'

'I know. Tell me about it. But you can't afford it and I'd be paying the fare to come over here anyway. And this way you'll see Jenna and Damien.'

Hard to argue with that, but he tries.

'See, I'm no long in the flat yet, is the thing. I don't know if I'm allowed.'

'I've spoken to your key worker and she says it's fine.'

He winces at Robbie using the word.

'Fucking hell. Da, I'm only talking about a couple of weeks, it's not like I'm asking you to come out and live with us.'

'No, course, I know that. Just it's a big thing, is all. I'll need to think about it.'

It is decided but, and he knows it.

The next few days he is thinking about it constantly, sitting in the flat or on one of the afternoon walks, worrying. Guilt, money, the whole caboodle. An agity excitement that breaks through but when he imagines being there. Seeing the grandwean – although of course he understands well enough that part of that is because Damien is too young to understand any of what's happened. Unlike his maw. He is nervous about the thought of seeing her, what she must think, all this time that Robbie has been gone from them because of him. If he could be employed by then, it would be easier. Obviously he couldn't afford the flight still, but maybe he wouldn't feel like such a bloody leech – he'd be able to pay for things when he's out there. It isn't looking too rosy though, the job search. It's enough of a struggle convincing them that he is a reliable, time-keeping, non-bevvied type of individual, let alone that he's qualified for anything. He goes into the office and sits waiting for his turn, never with the least expectation any more that anything will come of it.

One afternoon when he is returned from a hailstorm, there is a flashing red light on the telephone. It takes him a while retrieving the message, but when he has, it is Robbie, saying that he's wanting to speak to him so he'll call back later the evening.

When he rings again, Mick is in the middle of cooking tea. He turns the grill down and wipes the grease off his hands before going through to answer.

'Craig is coming,' Robbie says.

'Eh?'

'Craig. He's coming over here for Easter.'

There is silence on the line.

Jenna probably in behind, listening.

'Da? You hear what I said?'

'He know I'm coming?'

'He does. He needed a bit of arm-bending, but he's coming.'

. . .

'Da, it'll be fine.'

'The Highlanders as well?'

He can hear Robbie chuckling. 'No. It'll just be us.'

He goes on to explain the arrangements: where he'll be staying, the food they're going to eat, the trip down the coast they've got planned with Jenna's sister and her own baby. He doesn't take much of it in. Robbie says that he'll call again next week when he's booked the flights. He puts the phone down and goes back through the kitchen to get the grill turned off. The tops of his hash browns are burnt, but he plates them up as they are, with sausages, beans, and goes to sit down at the table and eat, as the hail starts up again outside, tapping and scratching against the window.

42

He is on the bus, the top deck, looking out for any signs of a toy shop. He'd tried down the high street but with no luck, so he decided instead to get a bus into the centre. Even now though, it's no looking likely. He gets down the stair and steps off. Wanders up a busy shopping street for a long time – clothes stores, fried-chicken shops, pharmacies, junk stalls – nothing. In the end, without any particular thought, he goes into a sports superstore.

It is a massive warehouse-type shop floor, mobbed out with swivel rails of trackie bottoms and luminous shirts. There isn't much of an order about it, and he has quite a difficulty getting through, squeezing between the huge bulging roundabouts of all this noticeably unsporty-looking clothing.

In one corner, where football and rugby boots are displayed on a wall, he finds a giant basket full of mini footballs. He rummles about through them on the off chance there's a Rangers one, but course it's all Chelsea and Tottenham and Man United, although he does eventually find a plain one, no team markings on it. Probably it isn't the best present for a toddler, but it's no bad. No bad at all. He decides he'll get it, and looks up the way, trying to plot a route through to wherever it is he has to pay. Radio station music playing loudly through giant corner speakers. A shop-assistant boy bent over, bundling up fallen heaps of shirts from the floor. Snooker cues, mounted on the wall like rifles. He snakes his way through, moving past the shop assistant. The clink of metal hangers going onto the rail – and an image comes into his head, distinct, vivid, the wife shopping. Out of nowhere. He puts a hand out to hold the rail, disorientated, needing to sit down. A buffit-step type thing by the wall, next to three cardboard cut-out snooker players with their arms folded, serious looks on their faces. He parks down on it and closes his eyes. Tries to hold on to the image. He can see it clearly. She is fingering through a line of tops, swivelling the rail around.

Her face. It is a study of concentration, looking down with a frown, a wee double chin pressing against her throat. Pulling out and discarding the tops back into the wrong place on the rail. He has started greeting. The suddenness of it. An overwhelming feeling of emptiness that he lets come over him, and he stays sat there a long time, minutes, hours maybe, fuck knows.

He opens his eyes. The cardboard snooker players stood around him and the shop assistant looking over, a grimace of confusion on his face. Probably he doesn't even know he's doing it. He gets up and wipes the eyes, gives the boy a wee smile. 'Don't worry, pal, I'm away the now.' And he gets walking off, squeezing hard on the mini football, to see if there's any tills through this bloody jungle.

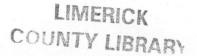

It is going to be another hot day. Already there are people putting up parasols and windbreakers on the beach, arranging cool boxes and pulling down trousers. There is not much wind yet, but the light breeze that comes off the sea is welcome as he jogs along the uncrowded promenade, past hot-dog vans and ice-cream stalls whose shutters are now being opened and awnings stretched out.

Where the promenade angles toward the town, he turns away onto the beach. He wipes his forehead, looking out over the sea: small still boats moored in the harbour, gently flapping banners mounted on buoys to advertise sea trips, hotels, the amusement arcade. The pleasing crunch of pebbles under his trainers. He continues down the beach, enjoying the stillness of the early morning. Seagulls. Waves sucking back through the shingle. A circle of pensioners doing knee lifts. Further on, along the base of the high wall – above which a line of bars and clubs looks out onto the sea – there is plenty of evidence of the previous night: broken pint glasses, cigarettes, fish-and-chip wrappings, a belt. He smiles, stepping up his pace as the beach arcs round and a long stretch of coastline comes into view – the pier jutting into the ocean, and, in the distance where the beach has ended, miles and miles of rocks and landslips and high, windswept farmland.

He has a sweat on now, continuing along the base of the town wall. He approaches a part of the beach where the pebbles thin out to reveal small patches of sand. On one of these, a short way ahead of him, there is a body reclined against the wall. He begins to swerve around it, keeping the same speed, until he is almost alongside, at which point he slows, turning to look at the man. Something unnatural about the way his body is positioned. Bent double; unmoving. It is fairly common on his Sunday-morning runs to see late-night revellers passed out on the beach, but this man is clearly homeless; that much is obvious from the state of his clothes. He is wearing no shoes or socks and his feet are hugely swollen and purple, a dirty red woollen hat pulled down over his face, which is bruised and blood-shot, a pink scar running down his cheek and neck and under his coat. He stops, just for a moment, and then begins again into a jog, following the brief wet curve of sand over a stream before it turns again to pebbles, and he continues on towards the pier, where the dim drone and convulsing lights of the amusement arcade have already started up.

Acknowledgements

I would like to thank Mary Mount and Peter Straus, my editor and my agent, for making it easy, even the difficult bits. Also to Joe Pickering, Jenny Hewson, and everybody else at Penguin and RCW, all of whom I feel very fortunate to work with.

For his early advice on the book that I thought this would be, thank you to Paul Chambers, and for what it did become, to Corin Pilling at the Cardinal Hume Centre, and Simon Hughes, together with all the staff and residents at St Mungo's Mare Street.

I am grateful to Bruce Biddulph for all that you shared with me, and to John Dolan and Jim Moohan of GMB for your willingness to help with my research. Furthermore, and especially, to Jimmy Cloughley and all at Clydebank Asbestos Group, whose aid and advice continue to support so many of the victims of asbestos and their families.

To my family, and the Tiptons; to David Vann (who had the idea for the title); and, more than anybody else, to Tips. Some of this book comes, however indirectly, from you. And thank you for helping me to make it better, even down to the bloody acknowledgements.